Solomon Snow
and the
Stolen Jewel

Solomon Snow
and the
Stolen Jewel

KAYE UMANSKY

CANDLEWICK PRESS
CAMBRIDGE, MASSACHUSETTS

Copyright © 2005 by Kaye Umansky

First U.S. edition 2006

Library of Congress Cataloging-in-Publication Data
Umansky, Kaye.
Solomon Snow and the stolen jewel / Kaye Umansky. — 1st U.S. ed.
p.   cm.
Summary: While trying to rescue Prudence's father from prison, Solomon, Prudence, the Infant Prodigy, and Mr. Skippy the rabbit find themselves caught up in the mad plans of the villainous Dr. Calimari to steal a fabulous and cursed ruby.
ISBN 978-0-7636-2793-5
[1. Friendship—Fiction. 2. Adventure and adventurers—Fiction.
3. Circus—Fiction. 4. Humorous stories.]   I. Title.
PZ7.U363Sol 2007
[Fic]—dc22   2006047331

2 4 6 8 10 9 7 5 3 1

Printed in the United States of America

This book was typeset in Columbus.

Candlewick Press
2067 Massachusetts Avenue
Cambridge, Massachusetts 02140

visit us at www.candlewick.com

For Yvonne Hooker, my editor, who never ceases to amaze

THE TOWN MUSEUM

is proud to announce
A MAGNIFICENT EXHIBITION

—• *for one month only* •—

No expense has been spared to reconstruct
the desert tomb of
THE FORGOTTEN PHARAOH
whose embalmed mummy was recently discovered

—• *and with it* •—

THE BIGGEST RUBY IN THE WORLD,
❧• THE FIRESTONE OF TOJ •❧

——

This perfect jewel, a plaything of princes,
is rumored to be Cursed!
No one dare touch it except its rightful owner.

——

YOU HAVE BEEN WARNED!

I Got the Tins Mixed Up!

❧

In which the Intelligent Reader
learns of the reduced circumstances of
Solomon Snow and his financially
incompetent parents. And in which
Betty is introduced.

So you're telling me the money's all gone, then?" said Solly. He was standing in the doorway at the time, just off to deliver a large wicker basket full of Old Mother Rust's unmentionables. "Pa took the last of the savings and spent it down at the tavern, and it's gone. That's what you're telling me, is it?"

"I wouldn't put it like *that*," protested Pa Scubbins. He looked a bit shamefaced, though.

"So it's not gone?"

"Oh, it's *gone,* right enough," agreed Pa. "I juss wouldn't *put* it like that."

"How would you put it, then?"

"He'd dress it up a bit," chipped in Ma Scubbins through tightly pursed lips. She was standing hands on hips, tapping her foot, glaring at her husband. On the table between them was an old red tin. The lid was up. It was empty. "*He'd* say he didn't know the red tin was the savings tin. *He'd* say he thought it was his ale money tin, which is green."

"Right." Pa nodded. "That's exactly it. I got the tins mixed up."

"How?" demanded Ma. "One's red; one's green."

"I'm color-blind."

"No, you ain't!"

"I am. It come on quick."

"Since when?"

"Since I got the tins mixed up!"

"You never got the tins mixed up! You know full well the red tin's on the top shelf and the green one's on the bottom!"

"Yeah, an' you put 'em the other way round!"

"I did *not*! Don't you go blaming me. . . ."

And so the argument raged on.

Solly didn't join in. He simply grabbed his cap, turned his back, and walked out of the hot, steamy kitchen into the early morning without another word. He didn't even bother to slam the door.

It had been raining in the night. Everything dripped. The vegetable garden was a sea of mud. The patch on the pigsty roof had come loose again. He could hear the pig snuffling around, squealing to be let out and into the hovel to eat scraps off the table. (Ma let it. Even though it trampled all over the washing, fought with the cat, and hogged the fire.)

Solly's eyes moved dully around, taking it all in. The shed was falling down, and so was the garden wall. The water pump was sticking again. The brake on the donkey cart needed replacing. Everything needed fixing.

Beyond the collapsed wall, drab moorland rolled away into the distance. Wet bracken, wet gorse bushes, wet stones. Wet sheep. Everything wet. Wet and broken.

And the savings gone.

He should have known, of course. Ma and Pa had always been hopeless with money. But the *savings*. Those last precious coins that he had insisted should be set aside for a rainy day—and they had even *agreed*! Pa had promised faithfully not to touch them, and Ma had said she'd make sure he didn't. He should never have believed them; they were notoriously unreliable.

Yes, it was his own fault. But he couldn't help feeling resentful. After all, it was his money. He'd earned it. It was a reward for something he'd done the previous year. The Business with the Spoon.*

Up until the Business with the Spoon, Solly had always thought of himself as the sort of person who enjoyed a quiet life. He lived up on the moors with Ma and Pa Scubbins, who ran the local wash-

---

*To learn more about this, the Intelligent Reader is urged to read *Solomon Snow and the Silver Spoon*.

ing service. He didn't really mind being a washer boy. It was all right. Hard work, but that never hurt anyone. He had never gone out of his way to seek adventure. When an adventure had come his way— one involving a silver spoon, a journey, and a very complicated quest—he hadn't enjoyed it much. In fact, he still had dreams about it. Horrifying nightmares full of fish, rabbits, orphans, chimneys, and an assortment of appalling weather conditions.**

Of course, it hadn't been *all* bad. At least he had made new friends. Little Rosabella, an annoying six-year-old who sang awful songs in a traveling circus, always wore blue, and was known as the Infant Prodigy. Mr. Skippy, a dull brown rabbit who was the most pointless pet in the entire world. And Prudence, of course. Prudence Pridy, the poacher's daughter, eldest of nine, who lived down in the village of Boring and dreamed of being a writer. Not that he saw them much these days. But it was nice knowing they were there. They had made a good team, the four of them.

He heard a clopping noise and a snort. The donkey came wandering around the corner of the

---

**You really should read it, you know.

hovel, trailing her rope through the mud and chewing on a mouthful of wet thistle.

"Morning, you," said Solly. He was fond of the donkey. She had been a major business investment. She came with a cart and helped speed up the deliveries.

Betty. That was her name. At the sound of his voice, her ears pricked up. She swished her tail. Her sagging backbone straightened a bit, as though an invisible puppeteer in the sky had tightened the strings. Briskly, she clopped over to the cart and slowly backed between the poles. She knew the routine.

Solly tromped through the mud to deliver the morning feed. Betty leaned heavily against him, batted her lashes, stuck out a long tongue, and slurped at his ear.

Betty came from miles away—from the coastal town of Seaport. She was a wharf donkey, apparently, used to pulling heavy loads. A few weeks ago, Solly had bought both her and the cart on the spur of the moment when out delivering washing. She had come trotting smartly up from behind and overtaken him when he was wheezing up yet another hill with a huge bag of dirty linen. Rather to his own surprise, Solly had used the last of his breath to hail the driver and inquire if the donkey was for sale. The man (who had an air of the sea about him) had said yes, it so happened he was thinking of selling her and buying a horse. Then he had named an alarming sum.

"The cart's included in the asking price, I take it?" Solly had asked, staring doubtfully at the dilapidated box on wheels with two rough poles sticking out at the front and a stick for a brake. There was room for three on the driver's seat, which was a warped old plank with nails sticking up. "It looks a bit basic."

"Less to go wrong," said the man.

Solly turned his attention back to the donkey.

"She's a bit thin," he said.

"Small appetite. Cheap to feed."

The donkey stood with her head down, not looking at anything. Solly walked over and patted her neck. A cloud of dust flew up. The donkey jerked her head up and looked at him. She had old, soft brown eyes. They looked—wistful.

"What's her name?"

"Don't have one."

Solly was shocked. Everyone deserved a name.

"I'll take her," he said firmly. "She'll be an asset to the laundry business. I shall call her Betty."

And that was that. Luckily, he had the reward money with him, twisted in a dirty old cloth thrust deep in his trouser pocket. At that time, he didn't quite trust Ma's tin system. (And rightly so. He should have gone with his instinct. Then he'd still have the savings. But he hadn't and he didn't.)

The man insisted on counting every coin, down to the last farthing, while Solly climbed into the driver's seat, carefully avoiding the nails, and picked up the reins. He couldn't wait to be off. He had never owned anything with wheels before. Or hooves. It was an exciting combination.

Finally, it was done. The man pocketed the coins and handed over the whip.

"No," said Solly. "I shan't need that. Come on, Betty. Giddyup."

Betty didn't move.

Solly said, "She's not moving. Ho, Betty, ho!"

Betty didn't budge. She just stood with her eyes closed.

"What shall I do?" asked Solly. "Do I need a carrot on a stick?"

"Ah," said the man. "That's one thing I didn't mention. You gotta sing."

"What?"

"Sing to her. That's how you start her up, see.

Donkeys are contrary beasts. They all have their little quirks. That's hers."

"Oh, great!" cried Solly. "*Now* you tell me! I pay all that money and now I'm supposed to *sing*? Any particular *style*?"

"Sea chanteys. 'What Shall We Do with a Drunken Sailor?' usually does the trick."

"Let me get this straight," said Solly slowly. "I've just bought a donkey who won't move unless I sing 'What Shall We Do with a Drunken Sailor?'"

"Or 'Fire Down Below.' She quite likes that one."

"I don't know it."

The man shrugged. He clearly couldn't care less. Well, why should he? He had his money.

"But I'm no good at singing," protested Solly.

"It don't have to be opera. You can stop once she gets goin'. It's just to get 'er started."

"But isn't that very inconvenient?"

"It is," said the man. "Why do you think I'm selling her?"

"Well, all right, then," said Solly. "If I must. But I still think it's ridiculous."

He picked up the reins again, cleared his throat, and, feeling terribly embarrassed, burst into song. He had a reedy sort of voice that cracked on the high notes. It did the trick, though.

"What shall we do with a drunken sailor?" sang Solly self-consciously, in his reedy voice. *"What shall we d*—whoa! Betty! Steady on! Aaargh!"

Betty's eyes snapped open, she gave a pleased snort, and they were off with a jerk that nearly dislocated Solly's neck. Within seconds, they were trotting down the lane at an unnervingly brisk pace.

And that was how Solly got Betty. He couldn't say he was all that happy about the singing business. He never set off in front of anyone if he could help it and always tried to park out of earshot. But life was a lot easier with the donkey than without.

"Hold still, Betty," he told her, hoisting the laundry basket into the cart and reaching for the harness. "Won't be long."

Betty happily nibbled his hair. She certainly looked better these days. She was fatter and cleaner. Her backbone still sagged, but there was nothing to be done about that. She was easy to feed and given to sudden, unexpected little shows of affection that were either appealing or annoying, depending on one's mood. She tolerated Ma and Pa but made it very clear she liked Solly best. Well, they spent a lot of time together. He had gotten quite good at harnessing her now. He knew where she liked to be scratched (behind the ears). Sometimes, on the road, when they had time, he let her stop and eat thistles.

Betty really enjoyed going on their delivery rounds—you could tell. She already knew the various routes. Especially the road to Old Mother Rust's, which led past Prudence Pridy's writing tree. The tree she always sat in when she was making up stories. The tree she hadn't been sitting in the last few times Solly had gone past.

A sagging shutter burst open to reveal Ma, framed in the window, holding a chipped cup. She was having a quick tea break from her fight with Pa.

"Where are you off to, Son?" she demanded.

"Delivery," said Solly.

"Who to?"

"Old Mother Rust."

"Well, make sure you come right back. I'm startin' the next wash and I'll need help wringin'. And there's a load o' sheets to fold. Don't you go stoppin' off for a chat, mind you. Like with that Prudence Pridy."

"No," said Solly. "Ha, ha—as if I would." He tightened the last buckle, sprang up into the driver's seat, picked up the reins, and said, "Right, then, I'm off. You can close the window now."

"Why? I'm your mother. I love to hear you sing."

"Just close it, Ma, will you?"

Sighing, Ma banged the shutter closed. Solly cleared his throat, took a deep breath, and burst into unmelodic song.

"Ahem. *Way-hay and up she rises . . .*"

And they were off, over the hills, and away.

THEY'VE TOOKEN MY PADDY!

❧

In which Solly suffers a disappointment,
then pays a visit to the Pridy cottage,
where there is a state of high drama.

Once they were off the moor and trotting along a winding lane, Solly felt anxious. Not far to go now. Would she be there, up in the tree, this time? He hoped so. He missed talking to Prudence. Tall, gawky, snappy, know-it-all, bossy Prudence.

He hadn't seen her for ages. The last time was when he had turned up with Betty in the new donkey cart. He remembered, because she had snickered in a slightly unkind way when he mentioned about the singing thing. She wasn't there the next day, and he hadn't seen her since, although he had managed to find excuses to go that way several times over the last week or two. Maybe she had a cold. That would take a while to get over—Prudence's nose being, well, frankly, considerable.

Perhaps the rain was keeping her indoors— although adverse weather conditions had never seemed to bother her before. Solly had seen her stride through blizzards. She was very hardy and self-sufficient. Well, she had to be. She was a poacher's daughter.

Solly was too shy to visit. The Pridys had few guests, except at night, when furtive figures slunk in and out, purchasing rabbits and pheasants at drop-dead prices. And Prudence had never invited him to visit. She said her dad slept during the day, but Solly knew better. It was because of all the stolen meat lying around. He could imagine it heaped up on the kitchen table. Gamy things in stew pots. Feathers everywhere. Big knives. Brrr.

Anyway, the Pridys had a chaotic household. Solly had seen Prudence's seven screaming sisters racing down the road on their way to Boring Village School, hair flying, pushing and shoving and tripping each other up. Prudence had stopped going to school, so there was no one to keep them in order. The boy baby, named Cleanliness, did nothing but scream and develop rashes. The thought of them all in a confined space with piles of dead wildlife around made Solly go weak at the knees.

Prudence would be in the tree today, surely? There was nothing he wanted more than a good old complaint session. He felt he deserved a sympathetic ear. If anyone understood about hopeless families, Prudence did. Her share of the reward money hadn't lasted two minutes. Mr. and Mrs. Pridy blew the lot on a once-in-a-lifetime trip to Town. Just the two of them. Prudence stayed behind to mind the kiddies. Three days later they came back with unsuitable presents for everyone and cheerfully announced that there was another little one on the way. Then Mr. Pridy had gone right back to the poaching. Prudence hadn't even seemed to mind. Just shrugged and said they deserved a holiday. She always fiercely defended her dad in particular. She wouldn't hear a word against him, especially since he had said she needn't bother to go back to school.

Solly wondered if she had finished writing the new book yet. He hoped so. People still sneered at her about that, saying that her dad shouldn't be so easygoing and should put a stop to it and make her get a proper job. Solly didn't, of course. He was keenly interested in the new book. Prudence had hinted that the hero might be a bit like him. Of course, she might have been teasing. You never could tell with her.

Yes, he was looking forward to seeing her. So much so that he could hardly believe it when he rounded the last bend in the lane and . . .

She wasn't there. The tree was empty. Again.

Solly's heart sank. He whistled to Betty, who came to a halt, steaming in the damp air. He pulled on the useless brake. It came off in his hand. Angrily, he tossed it into a bush.

How could Prudence not be there? Didn't she want to see him? Had he said something to annoy her the last time they met? She was so prickly, you had to walk on eggshells sometimes.

Solly thought back. What had they talked about the last time they met, apart from Betty? It was such a long time ago he could hardly remember. There had been no letter from the Prodigy; he remembered that.

Solly relied on Prudence to pass on the news when the Prodigy's letters arrived, because he couldn't read them. Not that they said much, being little other than rude demands for sweeties.

(They hadn't started off rude. They had started off as polite requests, in her best writing, on pretty blue notepaper.

Deer Solly and proodens how ar
yoo I am well so is mr. skippy
I wud be mos gratfull if yoo wud
send me sum sweeteez
lov Littel Rosabella

That kind of thing. It was the later ones that degenerated into raging abuse. The ones scrawled in black chalk, addressed to

The Meen Ones,
        Boring Village

And now even those had stopped coming. He was sorry about that. He was fond of the Prodigy, despite everything.)

Another thing about Prudence. She had promised to teach him to read, hadn't she? A promise was a promise.

Oh, *why* wasn't she there?

Anyway, there was no way Solly was going to go running after her. If she didn't want to see him, she didn't, and that was that. You wouldn't catch *him* chasing after some old girl.

A short time later, he found himself knocking on her door.

The Pridys lived in a tiny rented cottage on the outskirts of Boring. Their yard backed conveniently onto the woods where Prudence's dad went poaching. The front door opened directly onto the street.

It seemed very quiet inside, and there was no smoke coming from the chimney. That was strange. Normally, you could hear the baby's shriek from a mile away. And the screaming sisters were usually out front, pulling each other's hair and rolling in the gutter.

The rag the Pridys used for a curtain was tightly stretched across the front window. Maybe Mr. Pridy was in there, lying down in the dark, catching forty winks after a hard night's poaching. But as far as Solly knew, nobody ever bothered to pull the rag across for him. They wouldn't be out, would they? There was nowhere to go out to. Nothing happened in Boring. Odd. Could everyone have a severe headache?

Solly knocked again. Behind him, Betty shuffled her hooves and noisily chewed on a thistle. He was just about to give up and go when he heard dragging feet approaching.

"Who is it?" whispered a trembling voice from the other side. "It's not the landlord, is it?"

"Hello, Mrs. Pridy," called Solly. "It's me. Solomon Snow."

"It's snowin'?"

"No. Solly the washer boy."

"Go away. I don't want no washin' done."

"No, no. I'm not here about that. It's Prudence I came to see, actually. Is she busy? Can I speak to her?"

"No," said the voice, sounding choked. "She's in bed."

In bed?

There came the sound of a nose being blown.

"Why? Is she ill?"

"No. Go away."

"Could you tell her I called?"

"Who'd you say you were?"

"Solly Snow. Prudence's friend."

"Solly!" cried the voice. "Young Master Solly Snow! Well, I never! Why didn't you say so?"

Solly waited patiently while chains rattled and bolts were pulled back.

Finally, the face of Mrs. Pridy stared out through a crack. Unlike her tall, gawky daughter, she was a tiny, pale woman with bags under her eyes. She didn't have Prudence's unfortunate nose either. That came from her pa.

Today she looked worse than usual. The pins were falling out of her hair. Her eyes were bright red from weeping. Cleanliness dangled from one hip, fetchingly dressed in a cut-down flour sack.

He was a study in filth, from the tip of his sticky head to the toes of his mud-caked feet. Amazingly, for once he wasn't crying. His nose was running and his rash was flourishing, but his eyes were round and he was excitedly sucking his thumb.

"Where is everyone?" asked Solly. "Where are the girls?"

"In the front room. I've only just got 'em quiet. They've been up cryin' all night. Well, we all have."

In the front room? Nobody ever used the front room, unless someone died or got married. Something serious must have happened.

"How did you get them quiet?" asked Solly, fascinated. He wouldn't have thought it possible. Mrs. Pridy must possess some amazing mothering skills.

"I told 'em if they didn't shut it the big fork-tongued bog beast of the moor would come and eat 'em from the feet up."

"Ah," said Solly. "Right. That did it, I take it?"

"No. So I threatened to wake up Prudence. *That* shut 'em up. But where are my manners? Come in, Master Solly, come in."

So in he went.

Seven small girls huddled in silence on a battered sofa in the darkened room. Faith, Hope, Charity, Joy, Delight, Patience, and Grace. They were all dressed in cut-down flour sacks and their bare feet dangled. All of them were sucking their thumbs. Owl-like, their round eyes gleamed at him. It was very unnerving. Still. At least he didn't see any dead animals.

"What's the matter?" asked Solly. He stood awkwardly in the semidarkness. There was nowhere to sit. "What's happened? Why is Prudence in bed? Can I help?"

That's all he said. He wasn't prepared for what happened next.

Mrs. Pridy fell on his shoulder and burst into loud, trembling wails. That was the signal for everyone to join in. Eight small mouths opened wide, and the air was filled with howling. Cleanliness was loudest of all. He arched his back and let out a roar that should never come from a baby.

"There, there," said Solly. Helplessly, he patted Mrs. Pridy's heaving shoulder. "There, there."

"Oh, oh, oh!" wailed Mrs. Pridy. "Oh, oh, oh! Forgive me, Master Solly! It's just that you're the first one to show any sympathy! Nobody's come to call! No one else wants to share me terrible burden, though I notice none of 'em's averse to a nice fat rabbit on a Sunday!"

"What? Who? What burden?"

"Disaster!" cried Mrs. Pridy. "They've tooken him! Oh, they've tooken him! They've tooken my Paddy away and locked him up in the pokey! Oh! Oh! Whatever shall I do? I'll have to sell the kiddies' clothes and boots, and they won't be able to go to school for their dinners!"

More vigorous screaming from the sisters. Cleanliness flailed his arms around, giving his mother a nasty smack on the ear. Snot bubbles were coming from his nose.

"I'll take him, shall I?" offered Solly. "Why don't you make some tea or something? Why is Prudence still in b—oh. Um—yes. Hello, Cleanliness."

Solly's arms were suddenly full of raging baby and his jacket covered in snail trails of nose wipings.

"Tea!" exclaimed Mrs. Pridy. "Tea? There's a luxury! It'll be a long time before there's any tea! Now my Paddy's gone, and there's not a stick of firewood in the house!"

More howled agreement from the eight mouths.

"It won't be for long, though, will it?" Solly shouted over the cacophony. He jiggled Cleanliness up and down. Cleanliness smacked him in the eye. "Ouch! They'll let him out in a few days, won't they? They always do."

Well, they did. Mr. Pridy was frequently arrested

and carted off to Slopover, the next village, which was slightly bigger than Boring and boasted its own holding cell for local lawbreakers. He didn't mind much, Prudence said. He looked on it as a bit of a holiday. He claimed the food was rather dull, but the bed was better than the one at home. She said he whiled away the time playing checkers with the jailer, with whom he was on first-name terms.

"Not this time," wailed Mrs. Pridy. "This time, it's the County Jail. They've tightened up the law on poachin', so they said. The men comed yesterday in a black coach! They had his name down on a *piece of paper!*"

"Really? Wha—"

"You know what that means, when your name gets written down officially," Mrs. Pridy said, wringing her hands. "I saw it with me own eyes. *Patrick Pridy, poacher. Three years' deportation.* Prudence read it out. That's what it said. One o' those watchamacallits—dockermunts. Stamped, with a proper seal! They've tooken him to Seaport and they'll throw him in the jail, then they're gonna deport him to Black Island, where the real bad 'uns go! Oh, the shame of it!"

"There, there, don't get all ups—"

"Chains! Put chains on him, they did. My Paddy! His only crime was to put food on the table! Come with no warnin' they did, just as I was servin' up the squirrel what he'd brought home. He didn't even have time to eat it—not a mouthful! Chained him up, then tooked him away in the black coach! Oh! Oh! What'll I do?"

Two of the sisters—Grace and Delight—erupted from the sofa and hurled themselves at their mother's knees, nearly bringing her down. The others maintained a steady background chorus of banshee wailing. Cleanliness, apoplectic now, thrashed madly and kicked Solly in the stomach. Hastily, Solly put him on the floor, where he crawled off into the cold fireplace and began to roll in soot.

"I haven't slept a wink since it happened!" Mrs. Pridy went on. "The only one who's slept in this house is—"

"Me," said a brisk voice. "I needed a decent night's sleep because I won't be getting much for the next few days. Anyway, I'm up now. Everybody, stop that squawking immediately. I mean it."

Instantly, the squawking died down.

Solly turned around. Prudence stood in the doorway. She was wearing the brown shabby smock dress she always wore. The one with the bit of burlap sewn around the hem to make it longer. Her ugly straw hat was on her head, with a pencil sticking out in a mad sort of way. She wore a brown cloak and battered brown boots. It wasn't that Prudence particularly liked the color brown. That just happened to be the color of her clothes. The ones she wore were the only ones she possessed.

In her hand was a basket. It was very clear that she was on her way out.

"What you got your cloak on for?" cried Mrs. Pridy. "I hope you don't think you're going after yer dad! I'm not having you goin' to that rough old place Seaport on your own, and that's final! It's miles to the coast! It'll take days to walk there! Tell her, Master Solly!"

"Don't worry, Ma. I'll be fine." Prudence fixed her sisters with a Look that made them shuffle anxiously and try to stand in line. "You'd all better do what Ma says, or you'll be sorry. Patience, you're in charge while I'm gone, with Joy as deputy."

"Why Joy? She's too *sloooow*," whined Patience, hopping about on the spot.

"Aw, shut up," said Joy.

"The rest of you do what they say or else. And

Cleanliness'll be good for his mammy, won't you, Clenny? Prudey'll be back soon, with Pa." Prudence strode briskly to the mantelpiece and reached behind the clock. "I'm taking the rent money, Ma, to bribe the jailer. If the landlord comes, stall him. Hello, Solly. Can't stop now; bit of a family crisis."

Prudence scooped up two silver shillings and placed them carefully in a small drawstring bag, which she returned to the basket.

"Listen to her!" cried Mrs. Pridy. "Listen to her, the naughty girl, disobeyin' her own mother. Not even a thought of how I'll manage without her. And what if they won't take a bribe? They say once your name's down on a dockermunt, there's no goin' back."

"Nonsense," said Prudence. "Corruption's everywhere, even in the prisons. All jailers take bribes; everyone knows that. I'll get him out; don't fret."

"And supposin' they throw you in prison, too? They could, you know. Fer bribery an' corruption. Isn't that right? Couldn't they?"

She appealed to Solly, who didn't know.

"I'd like to see them try," said Prudence. She bent down, threw her arm around her mother's shoulders, and gave her a little squeeze. "I'll be back before you know it. With Dad. And maybe a stick of peppermint for everyone who's been good. Bye for now."

"Prudence, I . . ." began Solly.

Too late. She was gone. There came the sound of the front door opening and shutting, followed by footsteps receding down the street.

Eight small mouths opened. Mrs. Pridy's face was a mask of horror. Cleanliness looked anxious and held out sooty arms. At any moment now, the shocked silence would be replaced with hysteria.

"It's all right," said Solly hastily. "It's all right; don't let's get upset here. I'm going after her. Look, see? Here I go. This is me, going after her, out the door." He stepped quickly to the doorway, snatched off his cap, and gave a jaunty little wave. "See? I'm off. I'll catch up with her and give her a ride. Don't worry; I'll see that she's all right."

"You will?"

"Course. I've got a donkey cart now. Didn't she tell you?"

"Hear that?" cried Mrs. Pridy, wiping her tears. "Hear that, children? He's got a donkey cart! We're saved! Young Master Solly will sort out everything and bring yer sister home safe and sound! And yer dad, too, I shouldn't wonder."

"Well, I don't know about *that*. . . ."

"Oh, how can we thank you? Girls, line up over here and give Master Solly a kiss. Everything's all right again!"

"No, no," said Solly. "It's not necessary. If you really want to help, perhaps you could get a message to Ma and Pa."

"Of course, Master Solly. Our Joy'll do it."

Joy said, "No, I won't."

Charity looked up and said, "I'll do it, but I'll want paying."

"Joy'll do it and gladly!" scolded Mrs. Pridy. "What'll she say, Master Solly?"

"Tell them—just tell them—tell them I've been called away for a few days. Tell them to try not to burn the place down while I'm gone."

"Right away, Master Solly. You hear that, Joy? Those very words, mind you. She'll do it, Master Solly."

"But don't expect miracles," warned Solly. "I don't know that I can do anything about Mr. Pridy's—um—unfortunate circumstances."

"Now then, don't be modest. Prudence says you've got a head on those shoulders, and she don't say that sorta thing much."

No. She didn't.

"I'd better be off, then," said Solly. "I'll see myself out. Try to stay calm."

"I will," said Mrs. Pridy, smiling through her tears. "I feel better now that I know you're here to help us."

She sounded much happier now. It didn't help.

He had half expected Prudence to be waiting outside, but she wasn't. In fact, she was a good way up the lane already, really hurrying along.

"Hey! Prudence!" he shouted. "Wait!"

If she heard, she didn't turn around. He jumped into the cart, snatched up the reins, and burst into urgent croaky song. Betty's ears pricked up, she spat out a mouthful of chewed thistle, and she started off at a brisk pace.

"What?" asked Prudence with a little frown as they caught up with her. She didn't even slow down.

"Just exactly what do you think you're doing?" inquired Solly, pulling on the reins.

"You heard. I'm off to Seaport to get Dad out of trouble again."

"I'm talking about now. This instant."

"Walking. Why?"

"Well, stop. Get in. I'm giving you a lift."

"No thanks. Very kind and all that, but I hardly

think Seaport's on your delivery route. It's miles away."

"So I've heard," said Solly. "Hop in."

"No. I'm doing this on my own."

"I can't believe you're arguing about this. Hop in."

"No. Things could get nasty."

"So? I thought we were friends."

"We are. But it's my dad and my problem. I don't want you involved."

"Well, I'm going to Seaport anyway. I've always wanted to see the sea. So you might as well get in."

"All right," said Prudence with a sigh. She hooked a long, skinny leg onto the plank seat and swung herself up. "Thanks. But you're just the driver, that's all. When we get there, I'm doing everything else by myself. Agreed?"

"Agreed," said Solly, adding, "although I bet you'll be glad I'm here in the end. I bet I end up helping in all sorts of important ways."

"Hah!" said Prudence, settling down next to him with her basket on her lap. They drove on in silence for a bit. Then, because he couldn't help it, Solly burst out, "Where have you *been* the last few weeks? I came past the tree loads of times."

"Home. Where else? All the kids had stomach-aches, and Cleanliness is teething. You could have stopped by, you know."

Solly opened his mouth to protest, then shut it again. It was true. He could have.

"Have you heard from Rosabella?" he asked.

"No," said Prudence.

"I wonder where she is right now. Her and Mr. Skippy."

"I neither know nor care. Right now I've got more pressing things on my mind. Look, do you mind if we don't talk? I'm not in the mood. Just drive, will you?"

So Solly just drove. But he couldn't help feeling miffed. They were a team, weren't they? Him, Prudence, the Prodigy, and Mr. Skippy. Prudence was being particularly ungracious, even for her.

But then, she did have problems.

I WANT SWEETIES

෴

In which the Intelligent Reader visits
the circus and makes the acquaintance of
the Infant Prodigy and Mr. Skippy. And
in which Signor Madelini gives up on
gentle persuasion and resorts to bribery.

N o," said the Infant Prodigy. "I won't."

She was dressed all in blue satin and sitting on the bottom step of a pretty, blue-painted little caravan with blue frilly curtains on the windows. A brown, unmoving rabbit sat in her blue lap, staring straight ahead. Propped nearby was a large hoop with a blue ribbon tied around it.

Yes, folks! Step right up! The circus has come! After months on the road, Madelini's Marvelous Extravaganza has arrived in a field near you!

At that point, they were busy setting up. Gaily painted caravans were parked in a large semicircle, wagon-train style. All but one—a small, shabby yellow one with red wheels, parked away from the others, over by the far hedge. No one had watered the window boxes, so the flowers were dead. The door was padlocked. It had a forlorn look, as though it hadn't been invited to the caravan party.

The horses were wandering around nibbling at the grass, which was already turning into mud with all the activity. In the middle of the field, two sweating men were heaving on the guy ropes of a half-erected, heavily patched red-and-white-striped tent. As tents go, this was a small one. When fully up, it would be just big enough to fit the ring and maybe twenty people. The sweaty man shaped like a barrel was Zor, Strongest Man in the Universe. The sweaty old grizzled one was Bert, who helped with the horses.

A band, comprising trumpet, cymbal, tuba, and drum (Dick, Bob, Ted, and Carlo, if you're interested), was already running through a medley of oompa-ish sorts of tunes. Behind the tent, a dainty young lady in a tutu was just setting one satin-slippered foot on a tightrope slung between two poles. Her name was Miss Pandora Constantinople. (Her real name was Gertie Higgins, but nobody knew this.)

Elsewhere, an incredibly tall man on stilts was juggling five flaming sticks, an emergency bucket of water at his side. This was the Amazing Flambo, Eater of Fire (Frank, to his friends).

The stout woman in black sitting on the steps of the biggest caravan was Signora Madelini, the ringmaster's wife. She was furiously knitting.

Everyone was busy, except for the Prodigy, who was sulking.

"*Bambina!*" begged Signor Madelini. He had the unenviable job of being both ringmaster and the Prodigy's uncle. "Just tonight, uh? Be a good-a girl for Uncle Mad."

"No. Don't wanna be the dwarf." The Prodigy tossed her golden ringlets and looked stubborn.

"Rosabella!" pleaded Signor Madelini, snatching off his tall hat and running a hand through his hair. "*Bellissima!* Gimmee a break! I got-a problem. How I know Wee Willie Whippersnap gonna retire to grow the roses? I short of a clown; you know that."

"So get anuvver one."

"I try!" wailed Signor Madelini, waving his arms around. "I got-a posters up all over the county! Pinned-a low down for passing dwarfs to read! You think I not try? Come on, Rosabella. Ees only until we get a new one. All you got-a do is put on the costume and run-a round making the leetle cheeldren laugh. And get-a shot from the cannon. Easy."

"No. I hate uvver childwen. Don't wanna wear twousers. I want sweeties."

"You can't have sweeties, angel," said Signor Madelini, trying to keep his voice even.

"Why not?"

"Because I got-a no more! You eat-a them all. That-a why your buttons pop. Look at that preetty new dress Aunty and me buy you. Soon, it no fit. And what about your teeth? You wanna stay preetty leetle girl, don't you? So all the people love you when you sing-a your songs? You wanna beautee-ful smile, don't you?"

"Is you goin' to talk much longer?" inquired the Prodigy. "Cuz me an' Mr. Skippy want to pwactice our act." She planted a kiss on the rabbit's furry head. It stared blankly ahead.

"I am telling you, Rosabella," said her uncle sternly. "Uncle is telling you. You are not-a putting that rabbit in the act. I got-a standards."

"Then go away."

"Rosabella!" exploded her uncle, his patience finally exhausted. "You weel-a do thees theeng! Tonight you weel-a be the dwarf! I have spoken!"

"Won't!" roared the Prodigy, stamping her foot. "Not 'less I get sweeties! An' don't *shout*! If you shout any more, *I's gonna scweam!*"

"I not-a shouting! I just-a telling you! There are no sweeties!"

"All wight, a pwesent, then."

"I got-a no present! You got-a all the presents I got! Me and Aunty, we give-a you your own cara-van, new clothes, new parasol, new boots. How many presents you want? Rosabella, I beg-a you."

"No! Get Fwank to be the dwarf." The Prodigy nodded at the fire-eater, who was currently batting out flames, having accidentally tripped over his water bucket, fallen off his stilts, and set his trousers alight.

"But he six foot two! Only you are small enough to fit into the costume; you *know* that! We have to have a clown! The public expects one. Please. *Please,* darleeng."

Signor Madelini actually went down on one knee and wrung his hands. The Prodigy and the rabbit sat unmoving.

Signor Madelini decided to play his ace. There was nothing else to do.

"Rosabella," he said slyly. "I just-a remember. I got-a present for you."

"What?" said the Prodigy. She was trying to sound indifferent, but there was no mistaking the interested gleam in her big blue eyes.

"Ees-a surprise. But you got-a promise to be the dwarf. Will you?"

"Show me the pwesent."

"Ees een my caravan. Uncle's been saving it for a good little girl."

Eagerly, he strode away. The Prodigy looked

down at the rabbit in her lap, then picked him up and gave him a cuddle.

"There, Mr. Skippy," she said. "*That's* the way to do it."

Mr. Skippy stared into space.

The
PRIVATE JOURNAL
of
DR. CALAMARI

~ EXTRACT ONE ~

In which the Intelligent Reader

is offered an unprecedented

glimpse into the workings of

a criminal mind.

So, once again, here in my turret room in my lonely tower, I take up my pen. I have promised myself I will make a daily entry in my journal. It will be a useful record as well as allowing me to let off steam. In days to come, future historians will read my words and marvel at my fiendish cunning.

It's very chilly in here, now that the fire's gone out. Gross (my servant) hasn't gotten back, so there is nobody to bring up more wood. I'm certainly not doing it. There are 162 steps between me and the kitchen. Let's hope he returns by suppertime, or I shall starve. If I haven't frozen first.

I am tempted to warm myself up by unlocking my Cabinet—poring over my precious jewel collection always makes me break out in a sweat—but I must resist the urge.

Now to the master plan. It is making excellent progress. I have visited the exhibition at the museum three times now—once in my official capacity as a world-famous jewel expert, and twice more in disguise.

Needless to say, when I announced who I was, the museum received me with open arms. It was all good publicity for them. They fell over themselves to welcome me, and quite rightly, too. I didn't have to wait in line with the hordes; oh, no. They gave me a glass of sherry and a small, dry fish-paste sandwich, which I didn't much like.

I got a mention in the *Gazette*. I clipped it out and have it here. It reads:

Dr. Casimir Calamari, the celebrated jewel expert and notorious recluse, today visited the Forgotten Pharaoh exhibition. He declined to comment to reporters. He was given a private tour before returning to his remote coastal home, rumored to house a remarkable jewel collection.

And indeed, I was. The curator himself insisted on showing me round. A creepy little twerp by the name of Croup. I didn't like him.

"You do realize, Doctor," he slimed, "that this is a real feather in our cap? That this is the first time a small, provincial museum has shipped over and displayed the mummified remains of a real, live, dead pharaoh? Fresh from his desert tomb, no less?"

"Is that so?" I said with a bored yawn. I couldn't care less. Egyptian history leaves me cold. All that sand. All those camels. Not my sort of thing at all. I wasn't the slightest bit interested in the mummy, which by all accounts was disappointingly small and grubby. Oh, no. There was only one thing I was interested in. The jewel found buried with it. Now, that I *did* want to see.

They called it the Firestone of Toj. They claimed it was the biggest ruby ever found and was said to come with a Curse. What nonsense! At any rate, it was causing quite a stir. The papers were full of it. And, as a lifelong jewel collector, I was eager to inspect it.

Croup was full of information. Insisted on explaining all the security arrangements. Showed me into the main gallery, which was decorated to look like a desert tomb—flaming torches, sand on the floor, that sort of thing. Pointed out various jars of guts and old pots and broken ornaments and whatnot, none of which was remotely interesting.

"Where are the stuffed kittens having the tea party?" I inquired. "I rather liked them."

"Down in the basement," explained Croup.

"We moved it all, except for that large statue over in the corner, which was too big to shift. It's all Egyptian now. It's a theme, you see. Themes are the thing these days."

"Yes, well, carry on," I said. "I haven't got all day." If you've seen one chipped statuette of a jackal in a skirt, you've seen them all.

Bursting with pride, he then led me over to a dais on which were displayed two battered packing cases. These, apparently, were the ancient caskets. They were on the small side and not even gold. The paint job was terrible. The outer case was empty. The second, slightly smaller inner casket contained the mummy itself. It looked exactly like the pile of dirty old rags Gross keeps under the kitchen sink. Croup seemed to think it was wonderful, but personally I found myself distinctly underwhelmed.

"He's a bit on the short side," I remarked, staring in.

"Yes," agreed Croup sadly. "Poor Pharaoh Toj. A short king who led a short life. Reigned for a week, then got crunched by a crocodile. They only dug him up a short while ago, you know. Found him buried under a very small sand dune, which turned out to be an overlooked pyramid. That's why he's called the Forgotten Pharaoh."

"Mmm," I said, wearily tapping my foot and examining my pocket watch. "Fascinating."

"Isn't it?" he said, beaming. "So educational. But just wait until you see this!"

Scarcely able to contain his glee, he went scuttling up to the central pedestal and whipped off the covering cloth from a glass case.

"Come, Doctor," he urged. "Come and have a close look. I'll warrant you've never seen the like."

"I very much doubt that," I said. Well, I hadn't been bowled over up to now. My Cabinet is full of wonders, some acquired honestly, some not. Either way, it's all top-quality stuff. It takes a lot to impress me.

"It's cursed, so they say," said Croup with a little snicker. "The papers are having a field day with that. Of course, I wouldn't expect a clever gentleman like yourself to believe in such things."

I approached the case—and stopped. And looked. And saw—

The Firestone of Toj.

And from the moment I set eyes on it, I knew, without any shadow of doubt, that it must be mine.

How shall I describe it? Big. Big as a seagull's egg. And red. Redder than the reddest red in a world of really, really red things.

I pride myself that I didn't display a flicker of emotion. I even made out that I was unimpressed. That I'd seen bigger, better, redder rubies, and I didn't know what all the fuss was about. Then I left, pretending that I had other, more important things to do.

My subsequent, undercover visits to the museum have been most useful. Muffled in a large cape and wearing a blond mustache, I have mingled with the crowds and studied the whole thing from every aspect. I know it can be done. It is a bold scheme, but clever— very clever, though I say so myself. Oh, yes. Nothing has been overlooked. All I now need is:

1. Nerves of steel
2. Icy determination
3. A clear, cool head
4. A bent* dwarf

*By "bent," I am referring to villainy. Not physically hunched. Although, of course, he must be flexible.

I already possess excellent nerves and am certainly determined. I am working on the clear, cool head, but sometimes, I confess, I find it hard to contain my excitement when so much is at stake.

Oh, how I want the Firestone of Toj! Its rightful place is here, in my Cabinet, among my other trophies, shining for my eyes only! And why not? I am the world's expert, am I not? I've got the degrees and everything. Only I can appreciate its matchless beauty! I want it, I want it, I—

Must pause here. Am drooling and have gone all dizzy.

Opened the window. Better now. To continue.

Obtaining the dwarf is proving tricky. For the past week, Gross has been out trolling the countryside, but no luck so far. I have told him to haunt low dives, rough taverns, jailhouses, circuses. The sorts of places where bent dwarfs might gather. You would think the world would be awash with the little fellows, but apparently not.

It would be quicker to do it myself. But I can't. I must step back in this affair. I have my reputation to consider. I can't afford a whiff of scandal. I shall be the mastermind in the shadows. Then, if things go wrong, I can deny everything and let Gross take the blame. Besides, traveling around the countryside on a dwarf hunt in this weather holds little appeal.

Anyway, Gross had better come up with the goods soon. In a matter of days, the exhibition will close, the Firestone will return to Egypt, and we will have missed our chance. . . .

No. I must not think that way. That way lies madness. I will stay positive. I am confident that Gross will come shuffling in at any minute, armed with a dwarf short list.

Meanwhile, all I do now is wait.

ON THE ROAD

୬

In which Solly learns a thing or two
about literature, ancient history, and
geography, whether he wants to or not,
and Betty eats a thistle.

S o how are you getting on with the book?" inquired Solly.

"What?" said Prudence, staring at the passing scenery, which consisted of two tall hedges and little else.

A watery sun hung high in the sky. They were rattling along a narrow lane at a slow, steady pace. The cart was heavier for Betty to pull now that Prudence was in the passenger seat. She was sunk into herself, still not talking.

"The book you're writing. How's it coming along?"

"Oh, *that*." Prudence gave a disparaging sniff. "It's not. I got bored with it and threw it away."

"*Threw it away?* After all that *work*?"

"So? Who cares? It was rubbish anyway. I've started another one. I'm into detective stories now."

"What's a de—What's that?"

"Well, a dastardly crime gets committed. Usually, something gets stolen, like in *The Mysterious Case of the Missing Diamond Necklace*."

"The what?"

"*The Mysterious Case of the Missing Diamond Necklace.* It's a book I'm reading. I've got it in my basket. There are clues, like footprints or mysterious noises in the night. The detective is the brainy person who comes along and gathers everyone in the library and tells them who did it."

"Who did do it?"

"Ah, that's the beauty of it. The reader doesn't find out until the end. The whole point is to try and solve it yourself, before the detective."

"Why? The detective's getting paid, right? Why should the reader do all the work? Anyway, I thought you liked action-packed adventure stories best."

Solly was a bit miffed that she had dropped the story that he had privately hoped might feature someone not unlike himself. It seemed that his moment of fame was not to be.

"Not anymore. I do wish you'd stop talking. I'm trying to think."

"Suit yourself," said Solly with a shrug. She really could be annoying at times. All right, so her dad was in trouble and she was probably feeling depressed. Still. You would think she would at least *pretend* to be glad to see him. He was offering support, wasn't he? Support and sympathy. And taking her on the long ride to the coast.

"I wonder what it's like by the sea?" he mused after a bit. "They say the sea's even bigger than Puddleford Pond. That's huge. It takes over half an hour to walk round it. Have you ever walked round Puddleford Pond?"

"No."

"Well, it's huge. But not as huge as the sea. They say the sea goes on forever. I bet it's deep. Well, some of the ships that go on it are bigger than houses, so they say. How do you think big ships stay up, being so heavy?"

"I don't know. Who cares? Look, just stop going on about the sea, would you? Sea this, sea that. It's not *your* dad who's being deported over it."

"True," said Solly. A little mental picture flickered in his mind of Pa being carried up the gangplank in his chair with a pint of ale in one hand and his pipe in another. "Sorry. But he won't be, will he? Because you're going to bribe them to let him out. Right?"

Prudence bit her lip, then finally said, "I think it might be more complicated than that."

"That's not what you said to your ma. You made it sound easy."

"Only to stop her from panicking. Look! What's that?"

She pointed. A large poster was pinned to a tree up ahead. Solly pulled on the reins, and Betty slowed to a halt.

"What's it say?" asked Solly hopelessly.

"*The Town Museum,*" read Prudence, "*is proud to announce a magnificent*—oh, right. It's about the Forgotten Pharaoh exhibition. Some old mummy they've dug up and put on display for the paying public."

"Whose mummy?" cried Solly, shocked. "What did her children say?"

"Not that sort of mummy, silly. I mean a dried-up king wrapped in bandages."

"Oh, right." He went a bit pink. "Of course. *That* kind of mummy."

"You don't know what I'm talking about, do you?" said Prudence, raising a knowing eyebrow.

"No," confessed Solly. "I haven't a clue."

He spoke humbly enough. Well, it was true. He didn't know things, the way Prudence did. But he couldn't help feeling a bit resentful sometimes. It wasn't his fault his parents didn't believe in education.

"Well," said Prudence, "basically, mummies are

pickled dead people with their insides taken out and put in jars."

"Whaaaat?"

"Oh, don't worry—it was all a long time ago. Thousands of years. And miles away, in Egypt. That's a hot desert land overseas. It's called embalming. They did it to kings, called pharaohs."

"Are they the ones who dance in the woods?"

"That's *fairies*. Pay attention. The interesting thing is how they took out the brains. They got this little hook and stuck it in the nose and pulled out—"

"That's all right," said Solly hastily. "I don't need to know the ins and outs."

"You should. It's fascinating. Anyway, they've dug up this mummy of some obscure old pharaoh. Toj—that's his name. There was a jewel buried with him. They call it the Firestone. It comes with a Curse. So they say." She gave a dismissive little sniff.

"Really? What sort of Curse?"

"General bad luck or something daft. Who knows how these superstitions arise? I expect someone on the discovery team got dandruff. Or a paper cut on his finger. I can't believe you don't know this. It's in all the papers."

"I can't read, remember?" Solly reminded her

rather bitterly. "You haven't shown me how. Anyway, I can't afford the paper. Not now that Ma and Pa spent the last of the reward money. I haven't told you about that, have I? You won't believe it, but . . ."

And he told her all about the faulty tin system. He went on quite a bit, encouraged by the fact that Prudence was listening in silence. Well, he thought she was. Ten minutes later, he realized she was asleep.

Solly sighed. Being with Prudence always made him aware of how little he knew about things. He was ignorant of everything that was going on in the big, wide world. He knew nothing about museums or bandaged dead kings or precious rubies or detectives or clues or how to spring poachers from the County Jail.

It was a good thing Prudence did. Perhaps he should leave the clever stuff to her and just concentrate on the driving. On the other hand . . . why should he? He had a brain, didn't he? He wasn't just a walking stomach. Speaking of which . . .

"Prudence," he said, nudging her in the ribs, "what's in your basket?"

"A box of matches, a candle, a useful knife, and a book."

"Anything to eat?"

"Half a loaf, two pears, and a sausage," said Prudence sleepily. "And before you ask, I'm saving it for later, when we're *really* hungry."

"I'm really hungry now."

"Stop moaning and drive," said Prudence.

They jogged on in silence for a bit. Betty snatched a thistle.

Solly said, "So let's get back to the business with your dad. Are you saying that bribery might not work?"

"I don't know. I've never been to the County Jail. It won't be like the cell in Slopover. His name's on the official deportation list. That's serious."

Solly knew what she meant. Everyone knows that paperwork makes things a lot more complicated.

"But they'll cross it off, won't they? If you pay them?"

"I might not have enough. If it's anything like *The Tragic Incarceration of Percival Pickleby,* I'm in trouble."

"The what of who?"

"*The Tragic Incarceration of Percival Pickleby.* It's a book. Percival gets unjustly imprisoned and clapped in irons. His lovely niece Ammonia tries to pay his way out with her last farthing, and they laugh in her face and hang her for attempted corruption."

"How much have you got?"

"The rent money and my savings. Two shillings and sixpence."

Solly thought about this. No. It might not be enough.

"So what if it's not enough?" he asked. "Then what?"

"I don't know," said Prudence with a sigh. "Don't keep asking questions, Solly. I keep telling you, I'm working on it. Look, there's another one!"

"Eh?"

"Another poster on that five-barred gate. It's different from the last one. Slow down; I want to see what it says."

Sure enough, pinned low down on the gate was another large piece of paper.

DWARF WANTED URGENTLY!
Clowning experience essential.
Must be flexible enough to be shot from
a small cannon. Apply to Signor Madelini,
of Madelini's Marvelous Extravaganza,
currently playing just outside Little Backwater.

"Hey!" cried Solly. "That's Rosabella's circus! Imagine how great it'd be if we met up with her! That'd be a coincidence, wouldn't it?"

"One coincidence too many," said Prudence. "Things don't happen like that in real life."

The

PRIVATE JOURNAL

of

DR. CALAMARI

~ EXTRACT TWO ~

In which the good doctor

sternly quizzes Gross.

Finally! Gross has returned! He arrived a short while ago, looking a bit rough. A week's stubble and boots covered in road dust.

"You took your time," I said severely.

He hung his head and mumbled that he was sorry. Then he said he could do with a cup of tea. Does he think this is a café? I don't know what servants are coming to.

"Never mind tea," I told him. "Where is the dwarf short list? I wish to see it immediately."

Sheepishly, he handed me a small piece of paper. One glance told me that it was very short indeed. In fact, there was only one name on it. *Short.*

"'Short?'" I said. "Is this some sort of joke? Or is that his real name?"

Gross said he didn't know.

"And this is it, is it? Hardly a selection, is there?"

Gross admitted that no, there wasn't. Then he muttered some excuse about rogue dwarfs being in short supply and being lucky to find this one.

"That remains to be seen," I said. "I'll be the judge of that. We're only lucky if he proves to be the right man for the job. Where did you find him? What does he look like? Come along, man. Tell me everything you know."

It took some time. Gross's powers of recall are very basic. However, after quizzing him at great length, I must say that our Mr. Short sounds very promising indeed.

Gross first spotted him in Seaport, coming out of the County Jail. Gross describes him as a shifty-looking little fellow with a leather eye patch over his right eye. Gross tiptoed behind him at a distance, as I taught him to do, lurking in doorways and taking care not to be seen. (All those shadowing master classes I gave him were not in vain. Mind you, it was uphill work. Lurking doesn't come easily to Gross. He's not the right shape for it.)

First, Short made his way to the fish market on the dock, where he mingled casually with the crowd. There, Gross observed him steal a handful of cherries, a smoked kipper, two embroidered handkerchiefs, and three pennies from a blind beggar's collecting tin.

Most encouraging.

He then proceeded up the main street, helping himself to a pie cooling on a windowsill.

Better and better.

He then snatched an apple from the chubby hands of an innocent child swinging on a garden gate and strolled on out of town, kicking a cat on the way. Clearly a rascal of the first order.

Excellent.

Gross tells me that he has joined up with some sort of circus extravaganza a few miles inland. Apparently, they have a vacancy for a dwarf. There are posters up on trees all over the county, Gross tells me. Isn't it amazing? Suddenly everyone wants a dwarf.

Anyway. Gross followed him as far as the circus gates, then came hurrying back to report to me, as I had instructed him to do.

"All right," I said at the end of his garbled account. "All right, so Short's thieving credentials are in order. But is he flexible? Can he fit in small places? Can he climb a rope?"

Gross admitted that he didn't know. Of course, he could have established this by staying to watch him perform. I pointed this out. Gross said he thought I would be cross with him if he went to the circus and had a happy time. Which is true.

Mind you, if you're going for a job where you get shot from a cannon, the chances are you're pretty fit. It's a fair assumption Mr. Short is pliable.

The more I think about it, the more I am convinced that he is our man. Tomorrow, after darkness falls, Gross will return to the circus and put the proposition to him.

Will Short agree? Somehow, I think the bag of gold will convince him. I bet he's never earned that for a single night's work.

P.S. I have instructed Gross to tell Short only what he needs to know and no more. The bag is already packed, containing everything needed to do the job—floor plan of the museum, rope, ax, written instructions (in cleverly disguised handwriting), and a purse for expenses. The main payment will come later. Cash on delivery, that's the deal. When I get the jewel, he gets the gold, personally counted out by me, cunningly wearing my velvet gloves so that there will be no fingerprints. That will be the sum total of my involvement. Gross will do the rest.

P.P.S. I have been very thorough coaching Gross in what he is to say. I have impressed upon him to keep mum about the Curse. A pity it was spread all over the papers. I don't want our little friend to be distracted with all that superstitious nonsense—oh, dear me, no. Not with so much at stake.

Oh, when I think of the prize that so nearly lies within my grasp! To think that soon, very soon, it will be over. Those fools at the museum won't know what hit them. What a mockery I shall make of their pathetic security. I can see the headlines now: "Priceless Jewel Stolen from Museum! Police Flummoxed. Criminal Mastermind Suspected!"

But they'll never suspect me!

Miss Bunnikins

❦

In which the Intelligent Reader is
introduced to the Prodigy's new toy.
Mr. Skippy acts oddly. The Prodigy and
Miss Pandora Constantinople have a
conversation about the new clown.
Shorty considers his options and receives
an unexpected visitor.

The Infant Prodigy sat as usual on the steps of her little blue caravan. For once, Mr. Skippy wasn't in his usual place. He had been put to one side on the ground. He crouched like a brown lump, staring into space. To one side of him lay a carrot, which was odd. Carrot eating was the only thing that raised anything resembling enthusiasm in Mr. Skippy. He never, ever left them just lying around.

In his place, in the blue satin lap was—

Another rabbit. A toy one. A blue one. A magnificent, stuffed, blue toy rabbit, hand-knitted, using the softest of soft, fluffy wool. A rabbit that put Mr. Skippy to shame.

It was bigger than he was, for a start. Its ears stood tall and proud, with no sign of droop. It had two button eyes with stitched-on eyelashes. It had a shiny button nose. It had a smiley mouth. It wore an embroidered expression of happiness and a blue satin bow around its neck. It had a white cotton powder-puff tail.

The Prodigy loved it. Next to sweets, she loved rabbits and the color blue best of all.

"Look, Mr. Skippy," sang the Prodigy. "She's dancin'! You can tell she's a girl wabbit cuz she's got a bow. She's a little girl wabbit called Miss Bunnikins! Isn't she pwetty? Don't you love her? I do."

Mr. Skippy didn't move. Or did he? He might have given a funny little shudder—just a little one—but if he had, the Prodigy didn't notice. She was too wrapped up in her new toy.

"She's all mine!" crowed the Prodigy, her blue eyes shining. "All mine, an' I didn't even have to do nuffin'!"

She was right. The day before, true to his word, Signor Madelini had gone off to his caravan and returned with the ultimate bribe. For some weeks, his wife had been knitting it in secret. When she had finished, they had hidden it in a high cupboard the Prodigy couldn't reach. They knew her little ways. They were saving it to be used in just such a crisis as this one.

Triumphantly, Signor Madelini had produced the glorious creation from behind his back and handed it over.

Blue eyes agleam with greed, face wreathed in

smiles, the Prodigy had jumped to her feet, arms outstretched, spilling Mr. Skippy onto the hard ground.

And, just at that very moment, a hand had reached up and tugged at the hem of Signor Madelini's coattail. And a one-eyed dwarf with an eye patch said, "You the ringmaster? Need a clown, right? I can do that."

His name, he said, was Short. He had no references (they were burned in a fire) but claimed to have clown experience and said he could start right away. A delighted Signor Madelini had hired him on the spot. Which meant that the Prodigy hadn't had to fill in after all.

She'd kept the present, though.

"Dance, Miss Bunnikins!" trilled the Prodigy. "Hoppity hop, hoppity hop. Is you all tired? Does you want some dinner? Here. Have this. Mr. Skippy don't mind."

The Prodigy reached down, picked up Mr. Skippy's carrot, and pressed it to Miss Bunnikins's smiling mouth.

Mr. Skippy gave another, almost imperceptible little shudder.

"Did your uncle give you that rabbit, Rosabella?" inquired a voice. It belonged to Miss Pandora

Constantinople, the tightrope walker. She stood, stretching her legs and flexing her toes. As always, she was dressed in a white tutu and satin slippers.

"Yes," said the Prodigy smugly. "She's Miss Bunnikins. She's my pwesent for bein' the clown, 'cept I didn't have to cuz the new dwarf came. Isn't she beeooootiful?"

"Better-looking than that other rabbit of yours," said Miss Pandora Constantinople, stretching and bending on the spot. "That brown one that does nothing but sit. That Mr. Skippy."

"Oh, *him*," said the Prodigy carelessly. "I's been twying to teach him to jump fwough the hoop, but he won't. I don't care, now that I've got Miss Bunnikins. She's weally soft. I love her."

Mr. Skippy, sitting brown, carrotless, and forgotten on the ground, moved then. It was definite. He shuffled his feet, twitched his nose, and let out a convulsive little explosion that sounded like a sneeze. Neither the Prodigy nor Miss Pandora Constantinople noticed.

"I don't like the new dwarf, do you?" said the Prodigy. "That ole Shawty."

Both their eyes went to the small caravan parked away from the rest, over by the trees. The one that had belonged to good old Wee Willie Whippersnap, before he went off to grow roses. The one that now belonged to the new dwarf.

Nobody had seen the new dwarf since his frankly awful first performance of the night before. He didn't seem very sociable.

"What's he doing in there?" said Miss Pandora Constantinople, slightly disapproving. "Why isn't he out practicing? He certainly needs to, if last night's anything to go by."

"He's a tewwible clown," agreed the Prodigy with a sneer. "He's not funny, an' he don't even know how to put the makeup on. People was booin'. I had to go on an' sing again to calm 'em down."

"I know," said Miss Pandora Constantinople. "I was there."

"He was tewwible at gettin' shot fwom the cannon, too," the Prodigy went on.

"At least he *fit* in the cannon," said Miss Pandora Constantinople. "Let's give credit where it's due. It's a small space to squeeze down. He's fatter than Willie."

"But he said a Bad Word when his shoes was on fire, an' he said it again when he was in the air, an' then when he got tangled up in the catch net, he said it *again*!" said the Prodigy with gleeful disapproval. "Thwee times he said it. I heard him. Shall I tell you what he said?"

She whispered in Miss Pandora Constantinople's dainty ear.

"Good gracious," said Miss Constantinople, startled. "Really?"

"Yes. I wish Wee Willie was still here. I like him better than Shawty."

"He's a bit of a loner, I must say. Perhaps he's depressed," said Miss Pandora Constantinople, practicing a twirl. "About having only the one eye. And his poor old mother."

"What paw ole muvver?"

"Don't you know? Your uncle says he needs the job to earn money for his sick mother," explained Miss Pandora Constantinople. "Ah, the tears of a clown when there's no one around." She gave a sentimental little sigh.

"He's not depwessed," scoffed the Prodigy. "Howwible, more like. Howwible an' gwumpy. He fwightens little childwen. He kicked Mr. Skippy an' didn't say sowwy."

At the sound of his name, Mr. Skippy's floppy ears gave a little jerk. He hopped. Just once. One small hop, bringing him closer to the Prodigy's foot. She was kissing Miss Bunnikins and didn't notice.

"Oh, well," said Miss Pandora Constantinople, jumping up and crisscrossing her feet very quickly in the air. "We needed a clown, and now we've got one. I expect he'll improve in time. I must go and practice."

"Know what I fink?" said the Prodigy. "I fink that ole Shawty's not a weal clown. I don't b'lieve he's worked in circuses at all. I fink that's a load o' baloney, I do. I fink he's a bad dwarf, that's what I fink. I fink he's here to wob the takin's. An' I don't fink he's got a paw ole muvver. That's what I fink. I's gonna watch him, I is."

But Miss Pandora Constantinople had pirouetted away.

"I's gonna watch him, I is," repeated the Prodigy before suddenly returning her attention to her new loved one. "You an' me, we'll watch him togevver, won't we, Miss Bunnikins? Come on. Let's go an' play inside."

With that, she stood up, ran up the steps, and went into the caravan, shutting the door and leaving Mr. Skippy all alone and abandoned.

Much, much later, a large moon rose over the circus. The evening performance was over. The communal evening meal was over. The singing of songs around the campfire was over, and the circus folk had finally retired to their caravans.

Over by the hedge on the far side of the field, Shorty, the much-talked-about, one-eyed dwarf, sat in his undershirt and pants on the edge of the bunk in his tiny caravan, rubbing his sore head and considering his options.

His clown outfit—tiny red jacket with pom-poms, cone-shaped hat with a big flower, moth-eaten red wig, and daft puffy trousers—lay crumpled on the floor in a heap. A huge pair of spotty clown shoes, their specially reinforced tips blackened with gunpowder, lay in a corner, where he had kicked them.

Shorty was not in the best of moods. For the second night in a row, he had mucked up getting shot from the cannon. Both times, flying through the air with his shoes on fire, he had misjudged the landing and missed the catch net. Both times, the merciless audience had booed him out of the ring. Both times, that snotty little blue brat—the ring-master's niece—had rolled her eyes and loudly re-marked, "Talk about a tewwible clown," before walking on to sing a song about an angel and smugly demonstrating how to hold an audience in the palm of her hand.

Shorty disliked kids in general (a disadvantage for a clown), but he particularly disliked the blue brat. The trouble was, she was right. He *was* a terrible clown. Being funny didn't come naturally to him. He couldn't care less whether people laughed. The only reason he had joined Madelini's two-bit circus in the first place was that he was hoping to get a chance to make off with the takings. But every time he tried having a sneaky look through the window of the ringmaster's caravan, there was the blue brat, right behind him, arms folded and face contorted with dark suspicion.

Still. He had gotten his revenge. He had snatched her blue toy rabbit, the one she kept mooning over, when she was over in the tent blowing kisses to admirers. Shorty hadn't had any admirers, so he had slipped away early, swiped it off her caravan step, stuffed it under his clown jacket, and strolled on. Right now, it lay facedown on the floor, over in the far corner where he had kicked it. Later, when everyone was asleep, he would stroll across and stick it into the embers of the bonfire. That'd teach her to look down her nose at him.

Idly, Shorty picked up the evening paper and scanned the headlines. It was the first time he had read the news in weeks.

Just at that point, there came a soft knock on
the door.

"Yeah, what?" he shouted.

There was no response. It couldn't be the law,
could it? It was one of the hazards of Shorty's
lifestyle that the police were always on his trail.
Could they be out there now, creeping out from
behind trees, closing in, circling the wagon?

Shorty twitched the curtain aside and glanced
out. There were no circling policemen.

After a moment, the knock came again.

Shorty put down the paper, adjusted his patch,
and went to the door.

Like most caravan wagons, the door was split in

two. You left the top half open to get air in. The bottom half allowed you to go in and out.

Shorty unfastened the bottom half and peered out.

He saw the boots first. Massive, cracked, old ones, planted firmly on the top step.

And then it was the coat. An immensity of ancient black overcoat, which seemed to fill the world. Shorty's eye moved up the coat. Up past the straining buttons. Up, up, up to the strangely tufted collar, which appeared to be made from some long-extinct animal. And then farther up, to the head.

A huge man was staring down at him from the summit of the coat. He was bald on top but with strands of greasy hair at each side, hanging around his ears. His eyebrows were immense and dramatic. His mighty chin was covered in stubble. In one hand, he held a large carpetbag.

"Yeah?" said Shorty.

"Mr. Short?" rasped the giant in a hoarse stage whisper.

"Yeah, I'm Short."

"I'm Gross," said the giant.

"You said it, pal. What do you want with me?"

"I bin sent by my master to put a prop-o-zishun to you," said Gross. He pronounced the word very carefully, but with a hint of triumph, as though it had taken time and effort to learn and was worth saying properly.

"Who's yer master?"

"Ah," said Gross primly. He knew the answer to this one all right. "That, I am not allowed to say."

"What's the proposition?"

"There's somefin' Master wants. He finks you might be the one to get it for him. He'll pay you well for yer time. And yer hexpertise."

"Oh, he will, will he? How much?"

"I can't talk here," said Gross, looking over his shoulder nervously. "But I'll just say free—no, four—four words in yer ear."

Gross slowly lowered himself until his lips were on a level with Shorty's ear. Then he whispered, "One. Hundred. Gold. Coins."

Shorty's eyebrows shot up in astonishment. He said, "You'd better come in."

WHO'S INSPECTOR PARROT?

~

In which Prudence and Solly make
camp, and Solly learns more
about detective stories.

The stars look low. That means frost." Solly gave a little shiver. "Do you notice how it's always cold or wet or snowing when we're on these quests? It's never sunny, is it? Always awful weather conditions." He tossed another branch on the fire and hugged his knees.

"Shhh," said Prudence. "I'm reading. And it's not a quest. It's a rescue mission."

"Call it what you like—it's darned cold."

"Shhhhh!"

Solly inched his feet closer to the fire. His boots were pinching. Already, they were too small. He could almost feel his feet growing. Cold and hungry in the dark, with sore feet and Prudence ignoring him. Yes, this was a typical quest, whatever she might call it.

Solly wished the Prodigy was with them. She balanced things out. Besides, she might have sweets. It was a long time since Solly had tasted a sweet.

He shifted on the uncomfortably hard ground and gave a little sigh.

It was the second night of what was becoming an increasingly tiresome journey. Two days of empty, endless, winding lanes, enlivened only by the occasional farmhouse and the odd signpost pointing to THE COAST, but unhelpfully never saying how far it was. Two days of grumpiness and tiredness and snappy arguments. Two days of nothing but dry bread and a wrinkled pear, forced down with the help of stream water and the odd handful of blackberries.

Prudence hadn't helped matters. Her moods veered from glum silence to wild impatience. She got like that when she was miserable. She wasn't the type to cry. She just took it out on other people. She had shouted at farmers whose cows blocked the way and slowed them down. That made the farmers slow down to a virtual halt, of course (shouting at farmers never works, as everybody knows), but she never seemed to learn. She had moaned at Solly when he took the wrong turn at the crossroads and they'd had to retrace their steps. His argument that she was asleep at the time and that he was kind enough not to want to wake her up had had no effect. She just carried on moaning for ages, then she refused to speak. When darkness had fallen on the previous night and poor old Betty had finally ground to a halt next to a damp haystack in the middle of nowhere and Solly had announced that it was no good, he was going to have to catch a couple of hours' shut-eye, she had even complained about *that*. There really was no reasoning with her.

Solly shifted again, trying to get comfortable. The countryside being devoid of any convenient barns or ruined stables, at Solly's insistence they had made camp in a glade of trees a short way from the road. Betty had slurped noisily from a stream while they'd gathered damp firewood. It had taken ages to light. They had used nearly all Prudence's matches before it had finally flickered to life.

Under the cart, where it was relatively dry, they had laid out Old Mother Rust's thankfully clean(ish) washing to serve as bedrolls. Then they had cooked the sausage, carefully divided it in half, and eaten it. There were exactly two bites each.

And now it was over, the fire was dying, and Betty was munching thistles beneath a tree. Prudence was sitting with her back to him, nose in her book, reading by the light of the flames.

Solly glanced at her reproachfully. There was

something very annoying about sitting watching her read. The least she could do was make conversation. She owed him that, surely?

"Prudence," he said.

There was no reply.

"Prudence."

"What?"

"I wish we had some sweets. Don't you?"

"Yes. Now shush."

"Betty's happy to stop, do you notice?" said Solly. "She was really slowing down over the last couple of miles. I don't think she likes going toward the coast. Bad memories, I suppose."

"Mm."

"She was a wharf donkey, you know. She didn't even have a name."

"I know. You told me."

"Poor old Betty."

"Mm."

"I'm having to sing a lot more now, to keep her going. You could help me there, actually. I think I've got a bit of a sore throat coming on."

"You're suggesting I sing to Betty?"

"Well . . . yes."

"Forget it. Donkey singing is something I do not do. *Shhhh.*"

A little silence fell. Then Solly said, "What's happening, then? In the story you're reading?"

"Ah," said Prudence. For the first time, she sounded brighter. "Ah. Well, it's very exciting. The detective's just excluded another suspect. All this time, everything pointed to Billy Grubb having stolen Lady Lavinia Lovecraft's necklace, but he can't have."

"Who's Billy Grubb?"

"Her gardener. He's been acting suspicious all along."

"Then why did Lady Lavinia employ him? If he's suspicious?"

"She doesn't know he's suspicious, silly. Only the detective knows that."

"Well, as an employer, she should make it her business to find out," argued Solly. "Why can't Billy have done it, anyway?"

"He's got an alibi. That means he was with someone at the time of the crime. He was visiting his aunty on that fateful day."

"What's he doing visiting his aunty if he's supposed to be gardening for Lady Lavinia?"

"It was his day off."

"Maybe his aunty's lying."

"No. Inspector Parrot interviewed her. He clearly thinks she's an honest woman, and, having examined all the evidence, I agree with him."

"Who's Inspector Parrot?"

"The detective."

"Why is he called Parrot?"

"The same reason you're called Snow. Because that's his name."

"What's he look like, this Parrot chap? I'm guessing feathers? Sits on a perch, repeating things?"

"Don't be stupid," said Prudence. "It doesn't matter what he looks like. The important thing is that he's a genius with the most amazing brain. His deductive skills are quite brilliant. He knows a red herring when he sees one."

"A red herring?" said Solly, startled. First parrots, now fish. What did herrings have to do with this?

"It means a false trail. It's set up to put the reader off."

"Oh, right. But not brainy old Parrot."

"No."

"He knows his red herrings."

"Yes."

"Maybe that's why he has such an amazing brain. Because he eats a lot of fish."

"Oh, shut up, Solly!" snapped Prudence. She closed the book and stuffed it back into her basket. "Why bother to ask if all you can do is sneer?"

"I'm not sneering. I'm interested," protested Solly. "It sounds like quite a good job, being a detective. What makes a good detective, do you think?"

Prudence took her pencil from her hat and scratched her nose.

"Being good at noticing things," she said. "And listening to what people say. *Really* listening. That's important. And asking the right questions. And making connections."

"Hm," said Solly. "Interesting. Can washer boys become detectives, do you think? Or are they only good for being drivers and helping set up camp? I'd just like to know, that's all."

"I didn't ask you to come," Prudence reminded him tartly.

"No, but I'm here now. And all you can do is read some stupid story about some bloke with a bird name who goes around wasting his time on finding some rich woman's necklace. She's probably got loads of necklaces anyway, if she can afford a gardener. Old Parrot should concern himself with things that actually matter. Him and his amazing brain."

"Just listen to yourself! You're jealous of a made-up character!"

"No, I'm not."

"Yes, you are."

"I'm *not*," insisted Solly testily. "I'm just fed up with you having your nose in a book all the time. Anyway, what does it matter who stole the necklace? Why do you care? Your dad goes out stealing every night."

"Only food," said Prudence defensively.

"It's still stealing, though."

"Yes," said Prudence irritably. "I *know* that. I'm not saying it's right. I'm just saying he doesn't deserve to be clapped in irons and deported to Black Island."

"Except that he won't be, because we're going to get him out. Shouldn't we be discussing some sort of backup plan? In case bribery doesn't work? Rather than wasting time reading stupid detective stories?"

"Well, yes. I might come up with something, if you'd just shut up for two minutes."

"Well, maybe we could work something out together. My brain may not be amazing, but I'm not completely stupid."

"Look, Solly," said Prudence witheringly, "I'm a

writer. It's a writer's business to come up with ideas. Why don't you just stick with the driving and leave the ideas part to me, eh? I'm turning in."

And with that, she got to her feet, ducked under the cart, lay down on the spread-out washing, and promptly went to sleep.

Honestly, thought Solly. She is the most ungracious girl in the entire universe.

But she did have problems.

He sat hunched over the dying fire, listening to Betty moving around in the trees, wishing he could come up with clever solutions like Inspector Parrot.

The

PRIVATE JOURNAL

of

DR. CALAMARI

~ EXTRACT THREE ~

In which we learn more

of the doctor's cunning plan.

It's done! We have found our man! Gross returned last night with the welcome news! Short has agreed to everything! Hard though it is to believe, it all went off smoothly. Gross remembered all his lines. Short took very little persuading, particularly when told how much money he was getting.

"Are you sure you remembered to give him the floor plan?" I asked. Gross was looking far too pleased with himself. He works for me. He's not supposed to be happy.

Gross said yes, he had remembered to give him the floor plan.

"And the written instructions?"

Gross said he had remembered that too.

"And the ax and the rope and the candle and the generous purse for expenses?"

Gross assured me that everything had been safely handed over.

"And he was happy with the terms?"

Gross said yes, he was very happy with the terms.

"You didn't mention the Curse, I hope?"

Gross said no, he was very careful not to mention it.

So, everything has been set in place. Once again, all I can do is wait. My stomach is churning with nerves. I know I won't be able to eat any supper—but I'll order Gross to cook it anyway, just for the pleasure of telling him to take it away.

My watch says it's midnight. Now is the time. All being well, Short should be hidden in the larger of the two caskets and ready to make his move. His instructions were to catch the express coach to Town, buy a ticket to the exhibition, mingle with the crowd, slip into the casket when no one is looking, wait until dark, climb out of the casket, smash the glass case with the ax, grab the Firestone, make his way to the foyer by the light of the candle that I have thoughtfully provided, climb quickly up the large nude statue whose upflung arm so conveniently touches the skylight, smash aforementioned skylight (again with the ax), climb out, escape over the roofs, dump the evidence (ax, rope, candle, etc.), and be on his way back on the early-morning coach before anyone is the wiser. What could be easier?

And then, tomorrow night, Gross will return to the circus under cover of darkness, hand over the gold, and—oh, my fluttering heart—bring back the Firestone.

And that is the plan. Clever, eh?

BACK AT THE CIRCUS

❧

In which the Prodigy hunts in
vain for Miss Bunnikins and has
another conversation with
Miss Pandora Constantinople.

M

iss Bunnikins?" quavered the Prodigy pathetically. "Where is you?"

Dusk was falling as she drifted around the field, poking vainly under caravans and calling her lost beloved's name. Miss Bunnikins had been missing for almost two whole days and nights now, and, oh my, did everyone know about it! To say that the Prodigy had kicked up a fuss would be the understatement of the century.

At first, it had been all rage and temper tantrums. She had dramatically lain in the mud and screamed while everyone ran around in circles, holding out glasses of water, which she furiously smacked from their hands. She had held her breath until she went purple. She had jabbed with her little blue parasol at everyone within reach.

The circus folk had seen it all before, of course. The Prodigy specialized in tantrums, but everyone had to agree that this time it was a bad one, even for her.

Signor Madelini had called an emergency meeting. There had been a search of all the caravans. Well, all except Shorty's caravan, which was locked. On top of everything else, Shorty had suddenly asked for two days' leave to go to Town and visit his sick mother, leaving the Marvelous Extravaganza once again short of a clown.

The sawdust in the circus ring was raked. The band members inspected their instrument cases, in case Miss Bunnikins had somehow dropped in by accident. Despite everyone's best efforts, there was no sign of the missing toy.

The Prodigy, who was getting a sore throat with all the screaming, switched tactics and resorted to lying on her bed with her head under the pillow, indulging in some good old plain, heartfelt sobbing.

Judging it safe to approach, Signora Madelini had sat next to her, patting her hand and promising to knit her a new one. That wasn't good enough, though. It wouldn't be Miss Bunnikins. So everyone went off to search again.

And again, no luck.

When the time came to get ready for the evening performance and Miss Bunnikins *still* hadn't been found, the seriousness of the situation became clear. For the first time ever, the show had to be canceled, because the Prodigy shut herself into her caravan, declaring that she didn't care if she *was* the star, she was too upset to go on. What with that and no clown, Signor Madelini had no option but to cut his losses and tell the crowd at the gate to go home.

And now it was nearing the end of the second day and still the Prodigy remained inconsolable. All that mourning had taken its toll. Her eyes were red from constant weeping. She hadn't washed, slept, or eaten. Even her pretty golden ringlets were tangled, because she hadn't bothered to brush them.

"Still haven't found it, then?" asked Miss Pandora Constantinople, who was stretching her dainty legs against the side of her caravan.

"No," sniveled the Prodigy. "She's losted an' I don't know how. I's looked everywhere."

"Give up, then," Miss Pandora Constantinople advised. "It's only a toy, after all."

"But I love her! An' now I got nuffin' to play wiv!" wailed the Prodigy.

"Play with your other rabbit," suggested Miss Pandora Constantinople. "You've still got him, haven't you?"

"What, Mr. Skippy?" The Prodigy gave a careless shrug. "I fink he's wun away. He's just jealous cuz I doesn't like him as much as Miss Bunnikins."

This was very harsh, particularly as Mr. Skippy was within hearing. For two days now, he had been watching her from under caravans, but the Prodigy was too distraught to notice. He was currently huddled under the hedge, alternately staring into space and giving funny little shudders every time the Prodigy wailed Miss Bunnikins's name.

"Well, you'll have to get over it soon," said Miss Pandora Constantinople from the depths of a back bend. "We can't cancel again; it looks bad."

"I don't care," declared the Prodigy. "I's not doin' nuffin'. Not till I find Miss Bunnikins."

"I don't think your uncle will be pleased," warned Miss Pandora Constantinople. "He's already panicking because there's still no sign of Shorty. He promised to be back in time for this evening's show. He's cutting it a bit close."

"Good," said the Prodigy. "I hate him anyway. I hope he never comes back."

Their eyes moved to the empty yellow caravan parked all on its own on the far side of the field.

"I suppose we should be charitable," remarked Miss Pandora Constantinople. "He has got a sick mother, after all."

"So *he* says," sniffed the Prodigy.

"Well, I can't stay talking to you," said Miss

Pandora Constantinople. "I've got to get ready. And so will you, if you take my advice. The show must go on."

"Not wiv me in it!" declared the Prodigy. But Miss Pandora Constantinople had already cartwheeled away.

Over by the tent, torches were being lit and members of the band were ferrying their instruments across the muddy field, buttoning themselves into their red uniforms as they did so. The show was due to begin in less than an hour.

But the Prodigy didn't care. She was still staring at the yellow caravan. The only one that hadn't been searched, because Shorty was away.

The Prodigy's eyes narrowed.

He couldn't have. He wouldn't. Would he?

Yes. He could and he would. Why hadn't she thought of it before?

Two minutes later, she was standing on an overturned bucket, peering in the window. The curtains were pulled across, as always. But there was a small gap between them. The filth on the window and the angle made it difficult to see inside.

But down in the corner, there was something blue.

• • •

The door of the Madelinis' caravan crashed open, and a small blue tornado whirled in.

"What ees it now, Rosabella?" Her uncle sighed. He had enough on his plate without this. The clock was ticking, and there was still no sign of Shorty, who had promised faithfully to be back by sunset.

"He did it!" shrieked the Prodigy. "Shawty stole Miss Bunnikins! He's got her in his cawavan! I sawed her! He's a fief! A fief and a wicked wabbit-napper!"

"Rosabella, Rosabella," said Signor Madelini. "You got it all-a wrong, angel. *Eef* Miss Bunnikins is in Shorty's caravan, eet-a just-a because he keeping her safe for you. I expect you drop her by accident and he find her, uh?"

"No, I didn't. He tooked her on purpose. I know he did."

"Nonsense. Why he do that?"

"Cuz he hates me. Not as much as I hate him, though. Come on; I'll show you."

"Rosabella, you talking-a crazy!" expostulated Signor Madelini, throwing his hands in the air. "Uncle hasn't got time for this; he got a show to put on. When Shorty come-a back, you can ask him nicely."

"He's not comin' back," said the Prodigy. "He's

gone fowever an' I's glad." She held out her small hand. "Give me the cawavan key. I want to wescue Miss Bunnikins."

"I don-a have the key. Shorty got it."

"Then bweak down the daw!"

"What kinda man I be, breaking down-a poor Shorty's door? He got-a sick mama!"

"Bweak it down! Bweak it down an' get Miss Bunnikins or I's *wunnin' away!*" bawled the Prodigy, stamping her little blue foot.

"You see? You talking crazy talk again. Where you gonna run, this time-a night?"

"Somewhere where they's nice to pwetty little girls like me. An' where they gives me sweeties and does what I says! Not like you. You's *cwuel!*"

"You got-a have patience, angel. Wait for Shorty."

"But he's not comin' back!" howled the Prodigy, scarlet with rage. She stamped her foot again and waved her parasol in the air.

"Well," said her uncle, "well, that-a just where you wrong. Look."

With an air of triumph, he pointed through the window. The Prodigy looked. Sure enough, a small, familiar figure was hurrying across the field toward the far yellow caravan.

"You see?" said Signor Madelini. "Problem-a

solved. Now you can go and ask him-a nicely. Then get-a ready for the show, uh?"

"I'll ask 'im," said the Prodigy stoutly. "I'll ask 'im; don't you wowwy 'bout that." And she turned on her heel and marched out, the light of battle gleaming in her eyes.

"Wash-a your face, angel!" called Signor Madelini. "The audience want to see you looking pretty, uh?"

The Prodigy was already halfway across the field and didn't reply.

From his hiding place beneath the caravan, Mr. Skippy watched her go.

SHORTY'S RETURN

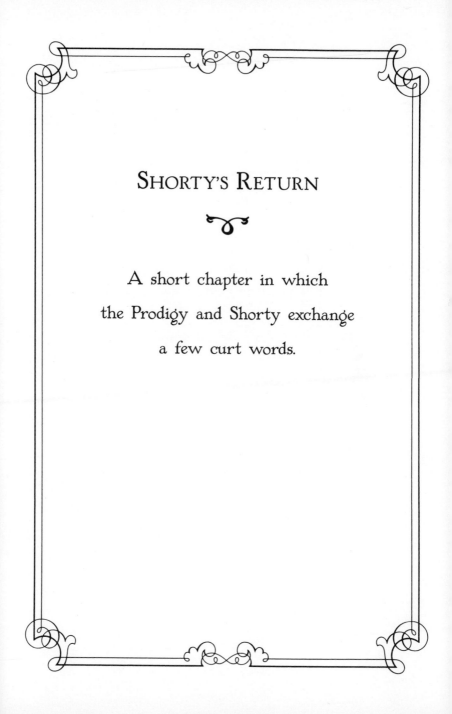

A short chapter in which
the Prodigy and Shorty exchange
a few curt words.

Shorty stepped wearily into his caravan, banging his head on the doorjamb and slamming the door on his finger. He gave a little shout and stuck the finger in his mouth. He hopped on the spot a bit and stubbed his toe on the stove. Then he tripped over the blue toy rabbit, which was lying on the floor, banging his knee on the edge of the bunk.

For some reason, he seemed very accident-prone. Ever since the night before, annoying little incidents had been happening. Nothing major — just a series of minor accidents and irritations.

A surprise attack by owls when escaping over the museum roof.

The drainpipe coming away from the wall when he was halfway down, spilling him into a pile of horse droppings.

Sinking up to his knees in the canal when trying to dispose of the sack of evidence. Being pecked by swans when scrambling out.

Tripping over and falling flat on his face not once, but three times, when hurrying to catch the coach, which was on the point of departure. Scraping his shin when leaping for the running board. Getting kicked by the horse.

Finding that the coach was already occupied by a cigar smoker, a pipe smoker, a fat woman with a basket of smelly overripe cheese, and a thin woman with a basket of overripe baby.

Everyone grumbling and refusing to move when he tried squeezing into the corner. Items of luggage falling on his head every time the coach wheel hit a pothole. Nobody else's head. Just his. Sitting for hours while canal mud slowly dried on him. That sort of thing.

Still. The job was done. He had gotten away with it. The robbery had gone according to plan, and he was in possession of the famous Firestone.

Shorty checked that the curtains were firmly pulled before taking it out.

There it lay, in his grubby palm. This was the first time he had had the chance to examine it properly. He had never seen anything like it, even in the fanciest shops. A perfect ruby, glowing with dark red fire.

What a sight. If it were his, he would look at it every night, bewitched by its red beauty.

No, he wouldn't. Who was he kidding? If it were his, he would sell it to the highest bidder.

How much would it be worth?

A fortune. Much more than he was being paid, that was for sure.

But tonight, when the evening show was long over and the circus folk were all tucked in bed, Gross would come and take it from him. He would never see it again. What a tragedy that would be.

Suddenly, there came a thunderous knocking on the door. Somebody making sure he was getting ready for the show, probably. Hastily, Shorty put the jewel safely away. He put it in the most excellent hiding place he could think of. Then he went to open the door.

Outside stood the little blue brat. She stood with her arms akimbo, glaring at him.

"Yeah?" said Shorty unpleasantly. "What?"

"Give me Miss Bunnikins," said the blue brat steadily.

"Dunno what you're talkin' about," said Shorty.

"Yes, you do. You got her in there, I sawed her fwough your window."

The blue brat was standing on tiptoe, trying to see past him into the caravan.

"You callin' me a liar?"

"Yes. You's a liar an' a fief, an' if you don't give her back *wight now,* you's gonna be *weally* sowwy."

"Oh, is that so?"

"Yes."

"Well, that's just where you're wrong," said Shorty. "I ain't sorry about a thing. 'Cept maybe for joinin' this two-bit circus. Push off, kid. I got to get changed."

And with that, he shut the door in her face.

Wight! thought the Prodigy. Wight. He's done it now.

Rosebud mouth set in a grim, white, determined line, she turned and marched off.

From the tent came the faint strains of the band tuning up. A small crowd was forming at the gate, where Signor Madelini was already stationed with his money box.

The show was about to begin. By rights, the Prodigy should be lining up to take her place ready for the grand opening parade.

But the Prodigy had no intention of doing so. She had more important things to do.

A short time later, dressed once again in the wretched clown outfit, Shorty emerged from his caravan. He carefully locked the door and hung the key around his neck. Not that anyone would find the jewel, of course. It was hidden in a safe place. Somewhere that nobody would ever think of looking. But nevertheless, it was just as well to be careful.

He set off toward the tent and what would be his last-ever performance. On the way, he tripped over his shoes and dropped his false nose in a muddy puddle.

It really was odd, all this bad luck he seemed to be having.

The Prodigy watched him disappear into the tent as the band struck up some merry circus music. Then she stepped out from the shadows and marched back to the yellow caravan. In her hand was a brick.

The

PRIVATE JOURNAL

of

DR. CALAMARI

~ EXTRACT FOUR ~

In which the doctor waits.

Gross has left for the circus, taking with him the bag of gold! He should be there by nightfall. If all has gone according to plan, in a few short hours Short will be paid off and the Firestone will be mine! Oh, the excitement! The Cabinet is all prepared. There is nothing to do now but wait.

Waiting is all I ever seem to do these days. I hate it. It makes me nervous. My fingernails are bitten to the quick. I keep worrying that something will happen to spoil things. Foolish, I know. My brilliant plan is flawless, supreme, the work of a genius. Short has only to follow my instructions. What could possibly go wrong?

A Confrontation at Night

In which the Intelligent Reader hears
an important conversation between
Shorty and Gross, and Shorty is forced
into an unwilling alliance.

What d'you mean, you ain't got it?" growled Gross.

"I mean just that. I ain't got it!" croaked Shorty. His voice came out in a strangled rasp because he was suspended in midair by the pom-poms of his scrunched-up jacket. "I bin robbed—you can see that, can'tcha? The kid's got it! Put me down."

The two of them were standing in a puddle of glass—the remains of the shattered window. Well, Gross was standing, head lowered and shoulders brushing the caravan ceiling. Shorty was dangling, the tips of his long clown shoes scraping the floor.

"Kid? What kid?"

"The little blue brat what works here. The ringmaster's niece. Little vandal went an' slung a brick through me window. Show's over, I comes back 'ere and finds the van in a jumble an' the rabbit gone. Put me down!"

Gross digested this information slowly. His brain worked through it, coming to a halt at a certain unexpected word. He tightened his grip and gave Shorty another little shake.

"Rabbit? What rabbit?"

"I'll tell ya! But you gotta put me down."

Slowly, Gross lowered his arm. Much to Shorty's relief, his feet touched the floor and finally he was able to suck some air into his lungs.

"Sheesh! What a night." He gasped. "I gotta sit down. I don't feel so good."

He crunched through broken glass, plumped wearily onto his bunk, and kicked his enormous shoes off.

"Go on," said Gross. "Talk. What was that about a rabbit?"

"I hid the jewel in the little blue brat's toy bunny rabbit! For safety! In case o' crooks!"

"But *you're* a crook." Gross scratched his head, a bit confused.

"I know! I *know*! And I knows their little ways. Takes more than a locked door to keep out a determined thief. Look, put yerself in my place. You've stolen a valuable jewel, right? You've got it 'ome safely. But I'm not comin' to collect it until later."

"That's the wrong way round," pointed out Gross. "*You* got the jewel. *I'm* collectin'."

"Yeah, I *know*. I'm just sayin' if I was you an' you was me."

"That's confusin'."

"No, it *ain't*. Look, try to follow what I'm sayin' 'ere. I'll do it slow. You're me. You've got the jewel. But you're not gonna leave it lyin' around in *plain sight,* are you? You're gonna hide it somewhere. You don't 'ave long, cuz you gotta get changed into your clown gear. You got a show to do. Now. What do you do?"

Gross bit his dirty thumb, frowned heavily, and wrestled with the problem. He wasn't good at thinking. He was paid to serve, not think. Doubtfully, he said, "Stick it in me pocket?"

"Stick it in yer pocket?" cried Shorty. "A priceless jewel? Are you mad? Think about it. You're getting shot from a *cannon,* for cryin' out loud! No; what you do is, you hides it somewhere innocent, where a burglar'd never think to look. Like in a little kid's stuffed toy. Which is what I did. I pushed it down the rabbit's ear."

"You'd better not be lyin'," said Gross.

"I ain't!"

"You might be. For all I know, you might not have had it in the first place. You *say* you did, but I only got your word for it."

He sounded rather pleased with himself. This was cunning thinking, for Gross.

"I *'ad* it," insisted Shorty. "I *'ad* it, all right? I did the job. You'll see; it'll be all over the papers. I 'ad the jewel and now it's gone. The kid's got it. They all think she's sulkin' in 'er caravan, but I know better. There's the brick—look. And look at the mess she's made! I'm not gonna do that meself, am I? And you can't get clearer than that message, can ya?"

They both stared around. The Prodigy had indeed made a mess. As well as the broken glass, she had ripped the curtains to shreds. She had acquired a tin of green paint from somewhere and poured it all over the floor. Scrawled in large, angry letters in red greasepaint on the wall was a message. It read:

i HaT you you feef i HaT
unKl too but I HaT you mor
I is ruNiN away to SEEpoRT
for sweeteez and nevr cumin
baK so ther.

"Master," said Gross slowly, "is not gonna be pleased."

"Well, no," agreed Shorty. "I can see that."

"My orders is to come back with the jewel. He's waitin' for it."

"Well, yeah. I take your point. But it ain't my fault, is it? I done my bit. All right, so it's *temporarily* gone, but it's not like you don't know where it is."

"He said I was to come back with the jewel," repeated Gross stubbornly. "It's more 'n my job's worth not to."

"So go and get it. Run on after her. She can't 'ave gone far. All you gotta do is catch 'er and get the rabbit off 'er. You can't miss her. She's blue; she's got a rabbit; she sings. 'Ow many others like her'll be walkin' on their own in the dark down a country lane? Go on; off you go."

"What if she won't give it to me?"

"Pinch her till she does."

"I don't pinch little girls," said Gross, sounding shocked. Then he added, "And you mean *we*. *We* follow and get the rabbit off the little blue girl. Togevver. You're comin' wiv me. You don't get the gold till I got the jewel. You want to get paid, don'tcha?"

"Well, yeah," agreed Shorty. "Yeah, naturally I wanna get *paid*. I just don't wanna hold you up. You'll go faster without me. Look, pal, I've had a hard coupla nights, I have. I ain't even taken off me greasepaint, and now I got to clear this mess up."

"But we're goin' togevver, right?" said Gross slowly and heavily. "Cuz if we don't get that jewel back, Master's gonna want some explanations."

"But I done my part of the deal!" argued Shorty. "It's hardly my fault if—"

His voice was cut off as a massive hand reached out and, once again, he found himself dangling in the air.

"We're goin' togevver. Right?" repeated Gross softly. "You and me. Right?"

Shorty had no option but to agree that, yes, indeed, they would be going together.

The Old Team

In which Solly finds out some useful information, Prudence reads the paper, and they meet up with an old friend.

Excuse me," called Solly. "How much are the cheapest buns?"

He was standing at the counter of a village bakery, feeling quite light-headed from the wonderful smell. All around were trays of crusty rolls and warm bread, fresh from the oven. There were cakes, too. Fancy ones, made with raisins and treacle and sprinkled with cinnamon and sugar. Big ones, small ones, some as big as your head. He could have eaten them all.

Prudence had grudgingly sent him in with a penny and strict instructions to buy two plain buns for their breakfast. They had been traveling since daybreak and they were both ravenous. She herself had remained outside in the cart. The morning was breezy, and she had found a discarded newspaper blowing down the street. Right now, she was anxiously thumbing through the pages, looking for the Shipping News section, which might contain information about prison ships and sailing times.

Solly could see her through the window. She glanced over at him and mouthed, "Hurry up!"

The baker came bustling from somewhere in the back, wiping his floury hands on his apron. He was fat and red-cheeked and had a cheery air.

"A penny each, young sir," he said. "But they come with currants."

"Just the one, then, please," said Solly with a little sigh. Half a bun each wouldn't be much of a breakfast, but they mustn't spend more than they had to. Every little bit counted.

"Just passin' through, are we?" asked the baker, wrapping the bun in waxed paper and staring.

Solly became aware of just how long it had been since he had washed properly. He took his cap off, ran his hand through his hair, gave a pleasant smile, and said, "My, it smells good in here. Yes, just passing through."

"Well, welcome to Piddling," said the baker. "We're on the map, you know." He gave a proud smirk and jerked his thumb. "We've even got our own sign at the turnoff. You probably noticed it."

"I did. Piddling. All those big letters. Very— um—grand."

"Aye, well, it's a grand little place. Decent. Law-abiding. I'm always telling my brother, Ted. A lot o' folk would like to live here."

"I'm sure they would. My nearest village is Boring. It's miles back."

"Boring? Never heard of it."

"No," said Solly. "No one has."

"Not on the map, then? No proper sign?"

"No."

"Bad luck." The baker paused in his wrapping and raised a sympathetic eyebrow. "I don't suppose much goes on in Boring?"

"No."

"Thought not. You'll love it here in Piddling, then. Young lad like you. We've got everything. That's what I'm always telling my brother, Ted. We run a best-kept garden competition. And sometimes we get a spot of cultural entertainment on the green. Folksinging. Poetry readings. Nothing too noisy. Jam making. There's a sewing club. Lots to do."

"I'm sure there is," said Solly politely. Then he added with regret, "But we're not staying, you see. We're on our way to Seaport."

The baker gave a sharp intake of breath and slowly shook his head.

"Oh, you don't wanna go *there*," he said darkly. "Rough old place, Seaport. That's where the sailors come off the boats, lookin' for trouble. Fights every night. And the baker's awful. Cheap as they come. Counts the currants in his buns."

"How do you know that?"

"He's my brother, Ted. Don't go to him."

"I certainly won't. I'm sure there are loads of currants in yours. How much farther is Seaport, by the way?"

"Far enough. Never go there meself. They got the County Jail there. That's where all the hard cases go, Ted says. The ones to be deported. There's a prison ship comes every Friday night for 'em. Takes 'em off to Black Island."

"Really?" said Solly, adding nonchalantly, "Every Friday night, you say?"

"Yep," said the baker, lowering his voice rather ghoulishly. "On the evenin' tide. The doors open and out they come, down Deadman's Passage, Ted says. All tied together in a line, with rope."

"Just rope? No chains or iron shackles?"

"Don't think so. I'm sure he said rope. Why?"

"Oh, no reason. I was just wondering what would happen if one of them managed to cut through his bonds and make a run for it."

"He'd never get away," said the baker. "Everyone turns out to watch when the prison ship comes. Ted says it's a fight to get on the dock; it's that crowded." He gave a disapproving sniff. "That's what passes for Friday night entertainment in Seaport. Throwing eggs at convicts. You don't wanna go there. That'll be one penny, young sir."

The exchange completed, Solly was just turning to go when he thought of something.

"By the way—what day is it today?"

"Friday," said the baker.

Solly climbed into the driver's seat and wordlessly handed Prudence her half of bun. Gratefully they both sank their teeth into the yellow dough.

"Any currants in your half?" asked Solly.

"No. Yours?"

"No."

"How much?"

"A penny."

"Rip-off."

"Mmm."

"Mmm."

It was only when the last crumb had been swallowed and the lingering aftertaste was dying down a little that Solly said casually, "Anything useful in the paper?"

"No," said Prudence disgustedly. She glared down at the crumpled paper lying on her lap, then crossly balled it up and threw it over her shoulder into the cart. "There's no shipping news. It's all about the robbery at the museum."

"Robbery? Why, what's been stolen?"

"The Firestone of Toj. That pharaoh's jewel, remember? Stolen the night before last. They're blaming kids. Or *a* kid."

"Why?"

"Whoever did it was small enough to hide in a mummy case. Waited until night, snatched the jewel, then escaped by climbing up some old statue—"

Suddenly, she broke off. Her sharp nose lifted, almost seeming to sniff the air.

"What?" said Solly.

"Shhhh! Listen!" hissed Prudence. She clutched at his arm. "Can't you hear it?"

Solly listened. At first, he could hear nothing but the far-off cry of a lone gull.

And then . . .

Then . . .

He heard it.

"I's got a little cookwy book my gwanny gave to meee . . ." trilled the Prodigy, soulfully batting her eyelashes. *"I's goin' to bake a Happy Cake, an' here's my wecipeee . . ."*

She was standing right in the middle of the village green, toe pointed, hands clasped around Miss Bunnikins, big blue eyes fixed on the heavens, doing her act. Around her stood an admiring crowd of villagers, hanging on to every note. Every so often there would come the clink of a coin landing in the opened blue parasol that lay at her feet.

"Take a pound of lovin' kindness, a spwinkelin' of joy, An' then you add the laughter of a little girl or boy . . ." advised the Prodigy in heartfelt song.

Her cake recipe really was going down well. A gang of village children had paused in their simple country game of kicking each other's heads in and were listening in rapt, slack-jawed silence. A farmer in a smock was openly weeping, dabbing at his eyes with his beard. A couple of snuffling housewives had pencils in their hands and were trying to write it down.

"A pint of Apwil dewdwops, a cup of golden sun,
An' then you puts it in a pan and bakes it till it's
    done . . ."

"A cup of golden sun," muttered one of the housewives. "Did you get that, Ada?"

"Happy Cake, Happy Cake, make one evwy day,
Give a slice to all the world an' keep those tears
*   awaaaaay!"*

finished the Prodigy, standing on tippy toes to hit the final high note.

"Hooray!" cheered the watching crowd. Well, those of them who could cheer through their tears. They clearly loved her. "Bravo, little 'un. Give us another!"

"Fank you vewy much," simpered the Prodigy, dropping a pretty little curtsy. "For my next song, I's goin' to sing you a vewy sad song called 'The Bwokenhearted Wagamuffin.' I know it makes *me* cwy. I hope it does you too. Ahem.

"Paw little wagamuffin, standin' in the stweet,
Doesn't have no bonnet or shoes upon her feeeee —"

"Stop!" came a sudden, sharp command. "Enough! Stop your caterwauling, Rosabella, and get into this cart *right now!*"

The Prodigy stopped in mid-trill. A strange

expression came over her face. Surprise, hope, mixed with a touch of anxiety, and perhaps a flicker of fear.

"Pwudence?" she gasped. "Is that you?"

The crowd turned as one and gaped at the small donkey cart containing a fierce-looking girl with a sharp nose and a brown-haired boy with a huge smile on his face.

"Solly!"

The Prodigy let out a delighted squeal that could be heard in the next village. Pausing only to snatch up her parasol, she raced through the startled crowd, hurled herself into the cart, and proceeded to smother Solly with kisses.

"I say!" protested Solly, blushing a bit, although still grinning. "Get off, Rosabella, will you? Mind my hat! Whoa, Betty! Steady on!"

"Solly! You's comed for me, like the pwince in the castle! I knew you would. I told Miss Bunnikins when we was walkin' in the dark. Solly'll come, you'll see, I said. This is her; she's new. I love her; don't you? She loves you too; look, she's givin' you a kiss. Don't you want to kiss her? Go on, kiss her. Oh, hooway! Now we's all togevver. Did you miss me, Solly?"

"No, he didn't!" scolded Prudence. "He didn't miss you one little bit. Why would he miss a vain little show-off like you? What have we told you about begging? The minute our back's turned, you're doing it again! Sit down. You're scaring the donkey and everyone's looking at us."

"I wasn't beggin'; I was doin' my act," claimed the Prodigy defensively, squeezing between them. "An' my pawasol juss happened to be on the gwound an' someone dwopped some money in it."

"How much?" asked Solly.

"Two halfpennies an' four farvin's," said the Prodigy, peering down. "Let's go an' buy some sweeties."

"We'll do no such thing!" snapped Prudence. "Drive on, Solly. She's getting on my nerves now."

"All right," said Solly with a sigh, picking up the reins. "Give me time, will you?"

"Well, come *on*. The natives are getting restless."

Indeed, they were receiving quite a lot of glares from the Prodigy's disappointed fans.

"Ain't she finishin' the song?" shouted the weepy farmer, clearly disgruntled. "The one about the poor little raggedy kid what's got no shoes?"

"No," said Prudence. "She is most definitely not. Solly, drive *on!*"

"All *right*. It's not you who has to do it. Just give me a *moment*. Ahem. *Way-hay and up she rises . . .*"

Betty was off.

"What's he doin'?" inquired the Prodigy. "Why is he cwoakin' like that?"

"Singing to the donkey," explained Prudence. "It's a new thing."

"Why have his ears gone wed?"

"Because he's embarrassed."

"Oh. Wight. Does he do it for long?"

"Just to get her started."

"Oh. Good."

"Yes, isn't it?"

They both exchanged glances and giggled a bit. Solly ignored them, and quite rightly, too.

The Prodigy waved to her fans until they were out of sight. Then she sagged heavily against Solly's side, stuck her thumb in her mouth, and happily murmured, "All togevver again. Like it's s'posed to be."

"Huh," said Prudence.

Solly said nothing. But the Prodigy was right. It felt good to be back together. The old team. Except . . .

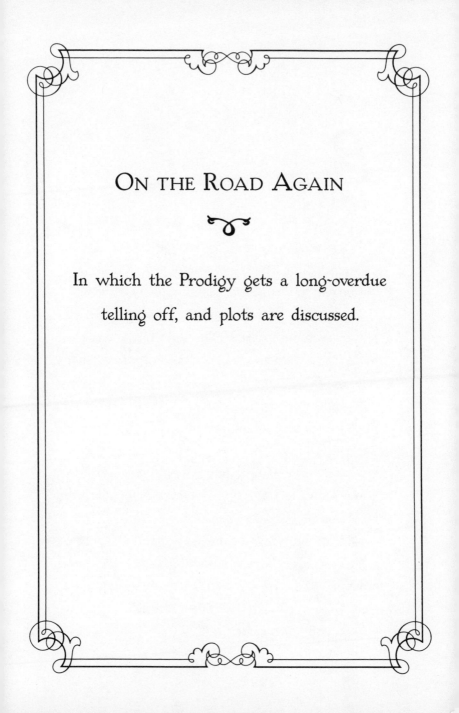

On the Road Again

In which the Prodigy gets a long-overdue
telling off, and plots are discussed.

*B*ehind?"

"Yes."

"You left Mr. Skippy *behind*?"

"Yes. What's the donkey's name?"

"Betty. Stop changing the subject. Are you telling us you left Mr. Skippy behind *all on his own*?"

Solly was incredulous. The Prodigy and Mr. Skippy were inseparable. The last time he had seen them, they were so close you couldn't have slid a ruler between them.

"Yes. Can I wide on Betty?"

"No! Who's looking after Mr. Skippy?"

"Don't know."

"You don't *know*?" Solly was almost shouting now. "You've left him on his own and you *don't even know who's looking after him*?"

"He didn't want to come." The Prodigy sounded a bit defensive. She was pouting a little. "He was hidin' away fwom us, wasn't he, Miss Bunnikins? He was bein' silly an' we didn't like it."

"So you left him behind!"

The Prodigy hugged her toy fiercely and dropped a kiss on the blue stuffed head. Then she looked up and said rather tearfully, "Yes. Did I do wong?"

"Do you hear that, Prudence?" said Solly. "Did you hear what she did?"

"I told you," said Prudence. "She's a monster. You're an unfeeling monster, Rosabella."

"Why?" sniffed the Prodigy, who genuinely didn't know. Back at the circus, she exercised a reign of terror. Nobody had ever pointed it out to her before.

"Tell her, Solly," ordered Prudence. "I'm too disgusted."

"Rosabella," said Solly severely, "Miss Bunnikins is a toy. She's stuffed. She doesn't have feelings. She doesn't *do* anything."

"Neever does Mr. Skippy!" wailed the Prodigy.

"But he's alive."

"Only barely, though," added Prudence.

"Look, whose side are you on?" said Solly.

"Yours, of course. I'm no fan of Mr. Skippy, but there are limits. Even *I* know a rabbit's not just for Easter."

"But I didn't get 'im for Easter!" sobbed the Prodigy. "I got 'im fwom a cage!"

"Even worse. If you decide to have a pet, you're supposed to take responsibility. You're supposed to love it forever," explained Prudence. "That's if you don't eat it, which personally I would have done before I got to know Mr. Skippy and realized how bland he would taste."

"Well, I'm very surprised at you, Rosabella," said Solly sadly. "I thought you loved Mr. Skippy."

"I do," moaned the Prodigy, rocking to and fro. "I *do.*"

"No, you don't," said Prudence scornfully. "You don't love him one tiny bit. You've abandoned him. You've chucked him to one side in favor of a stupid stuffed toy. Look at it, with its daft stitched-on happy look."

The Prodigy sobbed. She hid her golden head in Miss Bunnikins and sobbed. And sobbed and sobbed.

"Don't cry," said Solly. "Come on, Rosabella. Look, sing to Betty; she'd like that."

"You're cwoss wiv me!"

"I'm not." Solly didn't like making girls cry. Even when they richly deserved it.

"But Pwudence is!"

"Prudence didn't mean it. She's just explaining

you can't just abandon things when you get bored with them. You'll know better next time."

"No, she won't," said Prudence. "She's just a silly, spoiled little brat who's too used to getting her own way. She's beyond saving."

"I say," protested Solly. "That's a bit strong."

"Well, it's true. She's one of those hot-and-cold people who just love things to death for two minutes and then forget about them when something new comes along."

"I'm not!" quavered the Prodigy, rubbing at her dirty face with the hem of her dress. "I'm *nooooot!* I do love Mr. Skippy, I do! But the new dwarf didn't take *him*—he tooked Miss Bunnikins an' I'd only just got her an' Uncle didn't b'lieve me an' he wouldn't bweak the door in an' it made me cwoss so I got the bwick an' bwoke the glass an' wescued Miss Bunnikins an' wunned away to teach 'em all a lesson an' cuz I wanted sweeties an' anyway I don't fink Mr. Skippy likes Miss Bunnikins vewy much an' that's why."

"Yes, well, that's all very clear," said Prudence.

"Start again," said Solly. "What was all that about dwarfs and bricks? Go slower this time. Tell us how you got here, from the beginning."

"Well," said the Prodigy, "well, Wee Willie Whippersnap wetired to gwow woses an' we didn't have a clown. . . ."

And she told the whole story from start to finish. It took a while, particularly as she added extra embellishments of her own, in order to come out in a better light. All the while, Betty plodded onward with a faintly reproachful air. The gulls were becoming more frequent now and the air had a slight salty smell.

". . . an' then after I wote the cwoss message I wunned away an' I walked an' I walked an' my eyes hurt an' I slept in a twee in case of lions an' I got my dwess muddy an' then I woked up an' I was hungwy an' I walked again an' I was lookin' for a shop sellin' sweeties an' I saw the Piddlin' sign an' I fought there'd be one but there wasn't but I did my act anyway cuz I's good at gettin' money an' then I was goin' to go to Seapawt an' buy sweeties an' wun away to sea an' be a little sailor girl an' then you came along. An' that's it," she said, peering anxiously into their faces. "The end."

"Good," sneered Prudence. "I've never heard such a ludicrous tale. Missing Rabbits. Rogue Clowns. A Child's Mindless Greed for Sweeties. You should sell it to the papers; they'd probably put it on the front page, instead of the Firestone of Toj."

"What?" said the Prodigy.

"You tell her, Solly," ordered Prudence. "I can't be bothered to talk to her."

"Somebody's stolen a famous jewel from the Town Museum," explained Solly. "It's all over the papers. It's not important."

"Why isn't it important?" the Prodigy wanted to know.

"Because it's irrelevant to what we're doing, and so are you," said Prudence.

The Prodigy rolled her damp eyes pathetically at Solly and whispered, "Why is Pwudence so cwoss wiv me?"

"It's not you. She's got problems," muttered Solly. He glanced uncomfortably at Prudence, who was all hunched up and glaring straight ahead. It was clear she didn't want to talk. But the Prodigy needed to know the truth.

"What pwoblems?"

"Her dad's been arrested. He's in the County Jail. Waiting to be deported. We're on our way to Seaport to get him out."

"What's depawted mean?"

"I'll tell you what it means," said Prudence bitterly. "It means they put him on a big ship and take him to Black Island, where he'll spend years breaking up rocks on a chain gang. That's what it means."

"Oh," said the Prodigy, sounding quite genuine for once. "Oh, dear. That's tewwible. Poor Pwudence."

She slipped her arm around Prudence's bony shoulders. Rather to Solly's surprise, Prudence didn't shake it off.

"There, there," soothed the Prodigy, stroking Prudence's arm. "There, there. How're we goin' to get him out?"

"I'm going to try bribing them. But it might not be enough. I've only got two shillings and five pence."

"You can have my sweetie money," offered the Prodigy, generous for once. "Then you'll have two shillin's an' seven pence."

"Thanks," said Prudence. She sounded like she meant it.

"When does the big ship sail?" asked the Prodigy.

"That's the trouble. I don't know. I hoped there might be something in the paper, but—"

"Tonight," said Solly casually. "It sails tonight. On the evening tide. Every Friday, regular as clockwork. The gates open and the prisoners are taken along this alleyway called Deadm—this alleyway leading to the dock where the ship's waiting. But first, they have to get past all the people with eggs."

"What?" Prudence shook off the Prodigy's soothing hand and jerked around to face him. *"Tonight?* How do you know all this?"

"Oh, you know. Just a bit of minor detective work. Kept my ears open and asked the right questions. I think I might be developing an amazing brain, like old Parrot."

"Pawwot? Whose pawwot?" asked the Prodigy, confused, but she was ignored.

"Tonight!" roared Prudence, clutching her bonnet and rocking to and fro. "It sails *tonight,* and you knew and didn't tell me?"

"I haven't had the chance, have I? The baker told me. I was waiting for you to finish the bun, that's all. And then Rosabella came along and her story took over."

"Have *you* got a pawwot, Solly? Where is it?" broke in the Prodigy, still confused.

"Can't you get this stupid donkey to move any faster?" demanded Prudence. "How far do we still have to go? Will we make it?"

"Course we will," said Solly. "We'll be there in

no time. And while we're about it, you can tell us what the rescue plan is. I take it you've got it all worked out? What to do if they refuse the bribe and do what they did to that girl in the book?"

"Ammonia," supplied Prudence.

"Yes, her. Suppose they do an Ammonia on you?"

"What?" pleaded the Prodigy, *really* confused now. "What? Who's Ammonia? Has she got a paw-wot? What?"

"Shush," said Solly. "Come on, Prudence, tell us. What happens after that?"

There was a little pause. Then, "I don't know," said Prudence.

For a little while the only sound was Betty's clattering hooves.

"I see," said Solly. "So we don't have a backup plan?"

"No. *No,* all right?"

"I thought you said you just needed time to think. You said if I just shut up, you'd come up with a plan. You said writers were good at coming up with—"

"I know what I said!" shouted Prudence. "Look, I've *tried*! I've thought and I've *thought*. I've been through the plot of every book I've ever read dealing with getting people out of jail. Dressing up as a washerwoman, the fake royal pardon, using teams of horses to pull out bars, getting the jailer drunk—you name it, I've considered it. I even *dream* escape plots. Last night I dreamed I tried bribing a team of specially trained hedgehogs to smuggle in a key."

"That's *good*," the Prodigy complimented her. She added interestedly, "Did they do it?"

"No. I didn't have enough money, so they threw me in hedgehog prison. I shared a cell with a weasel. I woke up sweating."

"You should have paid 'em in slugs. Do paw-wots eat slugs?"

"Oh, shut *up*, Rosabella. There's no parrot, all right? I'm just saying that none of it will work, not in real life. In real life, there'll be real guards. Iron doors, chains, keys, echoing corridors, *official paperwork*! They're not going to be taken in by a—a stupid cake with a stupid *file* in it, are they?"

Her eyes searched the passing hedges, as though the answer lay there.

"You can cwy on my shoulder if you like," suggested the Prodigy helpfully.

"No, thanks. I'm not a crybaby. I leave that to you."

"Meanie," muttered the Prodigy. But she didn't sound too put out.

"There ought to be a backup plan," said Solly. "It's crazy, putting all our eggs in one basket."

"Well, there isn't, and that's that," said Prudence. "The bribe has to work. I imagine there'll be a head jailer or someone. I'll go right to the top and deal with it in a businesslike but firm manner."

"She's no good at persuadin'," hissed the Prodigy in Solly's ear, just a bit too loudly. "She's too bossy; I seen her."

"I heard that!" snapped Prudence.

"Well, it's twue," insisted the Prodigy. "You are."

"I don't mince words, if that's what you mean."

"No," said the Prodigy. "You mince people."

"Rosabella! That's a horrible thing to say," said Solly severely.

"I's just sayin'," amended the Prodigy hastily, aware she had gone too far, "you's not good at makin' people like you; that's all I's sayin'. But I is. Look, I'll come in wiv you. I'll be your little sister. I'll sing an' make 'em all sowwy for me an' evewyone will love me an' they'll let your daddy go fwee. Easy."

"She's right," said Solly. "They'll listen to her."

"No," said Prudence firmly. "I'm going in on my own. He's my dad, it's my problem, and I'm doing it my way." She nudged the Prodigy in the ribs, gave a little sigh, and said, "I know you're trying to help. Thanks for the offer."

The Prodigy said, "That's all wight. You can hold Miss Bunnikins if you like."

"I'd rather eat glass," said Prudence. But she smiled a bit as she said it.

"Look, Prudence," said Solly, "about this backup plan. Funnily enough, I had an idea. About what to do, if the bribe fails."

"Hooway!" cheered the Prodigy. "Clever Solly. You see, Pwudence? Solly's got an idea."

"Involving what?" said Prudence.

"Well," said Solly, "if the County Jail's like you say it will be, with guards and keys and chains and so on, our best chance of getting to him will be in Deadma—in the passage that runs between the jail and the dock. Right?"

"Right," chorused Prudence and the Prodigy. Then Prudence added, "Although he's sure to be guarded."

"And we know there'll be a big crowd on the dock. So," went on Solly, "supposing we create a—

what's it called when you make a big fuss to get people's attention? And then do something clever when they're looking the other way?"

"You mean a diversion?" said Prudence thoughtfully.

"Right, one of those. Suppose we . . ."

And the cart moved on down the road as Solly told them his plan.

The
PRIVATE JOURNAL
of
DR. CALAMARI

~ EXTRACT FIVE ~

In which the doctor's nerves

really kick in.

Good news and bad news!

The good news first. Success! Short has done the deed! I have before me the newspaper, which is full of the robbery at the museum. The headlines are just what I expected. Shocking Discovery, Firestone Stolen, Police Baffled, Criminal Mastermind Suspected, and so on and so forth. Oh, what I would give to have seen Croup's face when he opened up yesterday morning to a sea of broken glass and an empty pedestal where the jewel should be. It was probably as horrified as the face of the newspaper boy when I opened the door this morning and nearly strangled him in my eagerness, thinking he was Gross with the jewel!

Which brings me to the bad news. I haven't seen Gross since last night, when he left for the circus. Pay up and collect. That's all he had to do. How long does that take? Whatever is keeping him? Could someone have robbed him on the highway? Has he had an accident? Fallen down a mine shaft, developed amnesia, been crushed by a meteorite, enchanted by fairies? All night I was up, pacing back and forth, running down 162 steps to the front door every two minutes to check whether the fool was back. I declare I didn't have a wink of sleep.

Gross! Gross! Where are you, you fool? More important, where is the Firestone?

ON THE TRAIL

In which the Intelligent Reader joins
Gross and Shorty, who are in pursuit
of the Prodigy.

T

wo figures—one big and hulking, one small and sullen-looking—came limping tiredly along the winding country lane.

Gross and Shorty were hot on the Prodigy's trail.

Well, not exactly hot. They were quite cold, actually, despite having walked all night.

At first the trailing had been easy. There had been a full moon and a sky full of stars. Plus, they had a lantern, borrowed from the caravan, which miraculously had survived the Prodigy's onslaught. Conveniently, she had stepped in the green paint she had thrown about in such copious amounts. Her small footsteps showed up clearly in the silvery light, leading off down the lane, heading south.

Gross had set off eagerly, moving with huge strides, head lowered to the ground, with the reluctant Shorty dragging along behind. After a while, the Prodigy's painty footsteps had faded to nothing, but even so there were clear signs of furious, indignant passage. When she was in one of her tantrums, her habit was to lash out with her parasol. She had left a miniature storm in her wake. The rutted lane was littered with scattered twigs and decapitated flower heads. Whenever the road divided, you just had to look for whacked hedges and trees with chunks taken out. She couldn't have blazed a clearer trail if she'd used a chain saw.

But, as the night wore on, her temper had evidently worn off. Either that, or she had gotten tired. There were now no signs of attacks on the blameless hedges. The road ahead lay empty and barren of clues.

That didn't stop Gross, though. He kept going south, with relentless, shuffling determination, and Shorty had no option but to keep going too. There had been no attempts at conversation. They both needed all their breath for walking.

And now a new day had dawned, and still they were walking.

"Can we stop for a minute?" begged Shorty, staggering to a halt.

He was having a horrible time. His hot, scratchy clown clothes were picking up hundreds of burrs. His bare feet were killing him. He was covered in road dust, which stuck to the greasepaint, which he hadn't even had time to remove. During the long night, annoying things had kept happening to him. Branches would swing back in his face. A cow had leaned over a fence and spat cud all over his trousers.

All this after hiding in a coffin, stealing a jewel, escaping from the museum, coming home, getting in a fight, dressing up as a clown, doing an unpopular performance, coming back to find his caravan trashed, then being half strangled by a gorilla with a mission. What life threw at you sometimes.

"No," said Gross. "Keep goin'. We gotta catch up with the little blue girl."

"But my legs are shorter than yours," grumbled Shorty. "Is that an oasis ahead or am I hallucinatin'?"

"Don't be daft. Keep goin'."

"Look, I'm worn out. I gotta sleep."

"We gotta get the jewel off the little blue girl," said Gross. "That's all I know."

"But the trail's stone cold. Kid could be anywhere by now."

"Seaport," said Gross doggedly. "That's where's she's goin'. We gotta get the j—"

"I know, I *know*! So you keep sayin'. We *will*. Just not like this." Shorty flopped down onto a nearby log and rubbed his feet while he spoke. "Look. Let's think about this for a moment. We're goin' about this all wrong. Supposin' she changed her mind? Supposin' she heard us comin' in the dark an' hid behind a tree? Then went home again? She could be back at the circus by now. Thought of that?"

There was a long pause while Gross thought about whether he had, in fact, thought about that.

"No," he admitted finally.

"Right. So we ought to split up. You carry on to Seaport, just in case, an' I'll backtrack. You know it makes sense."

"I dunno," said Gross, pulling in his upper lip. "I dunno what Master'd say."

"He'd agree with me," urged Shorty.

"I dunno," repeated Gross wretchedly. "I dunno."

"Who is he, anyway?" asked Shorty curiously. "This oh-so-secret master of yours? Important man, is he? Got a reputation to protect?"

"Stop askin' questions," said Gross. "I told you, I'm not allowed to say."

"I'm guessing he's rich."

"How d'you know that? I never told you that!" Gross's shaggy eyebrows bristled anxiously. "Anyway, I don't want to talk anymore. You're tryin' to trick me into tellin'."

"I know the type. Keeps his hands clean and gets you to do all his dirty work, eh?"

"Well—yers. Yers, I does that."

"Does he thank you for it?"

"No," said Gross.

"Pays you a good wage, does he?"

"No," said Gross.

"Oh, I see. He's got somethin' on you, right? It's a blackmail situation. You work for him for free and he won't tell the world your terrible secret. Is that it?"

"No," said Gross.

"Why do it, then?"

"You wouldn't understand," said Gross. "It's a faithful family retainer thing. All us Grosses are the same. Born to serve, see? Anyway, that's enough talk. I know what you're doing. You're trying to trick me into tellin' you stuff. Dr. Calamari said I wasn't to—oops!" He clapped a hand over his mouth and looked horrified. "I've said too much."

"Dr. Calamari, eh?" said Shorty thoughtfully. "That'd be Dr. *Casimir* Calamari, well-known expert in valuable jewel circles? Yeah, I've heard of him. So he's the one behind all this."

"Yers," admitted Gross anxiously. "You won't say I said so, will you? I wouldn't want to get fired."

"Why not? Get another master. Or be like me. Work for yourself."

"Oh, no," said Gross, shocked. "What, lie in coffins and creep about in the dark and steal valuable pharaoh's rubies? Wiv Curses on 'em? Ah— *blast*! I've done it again!"

"What was that about a Curse?"

"Did I say Curse? That was a slip of the tongue. Look, that's enough talkin'. You're not getting no more out of me. Come on. You're dawdling. Keep those legs movin'."

SEAPORT

❧

In which Prudence swings into action,
with expected results. The Prodigy
misses Mr. Skippy, and preparations
are made for the backup plan.

The Head Jailer sat in his private office with his feet up on the desk. He was leaning back in his chair, taking large slurps from a mug full of strong tea.

The Head Jailer's name was Henry Stumping, and he loved his job. He was a vision in studded black leather, as all good jailers should be. He had the stubble and the greasy ponytail. He also had the warm office, the teapot, and the clipboard. Oh, and the biggest stick. He answered to no one, did more or less what he liked, drank a lot of tea, shouted at the prisoners, and bossed the lesser guards around. It was the job of his dreams. He was a happy man.

Henry had been down in the cells taunting prisoners all day and was taking a well-earned break. He was on his third mug of tea, idly picking cookie crumbs out of his teeth with one of the keys on his ring and reading the paper, which was full of exciting news about a daring robbery at the Town Museum. Over his head, a long chain of keys hung from hooks hammered into the stone walls.

There were keys for everything. Big, rusty ones. Small, secret ones. Really important ones, like the key to the supply closet and the pantry. All were neatly labeled. Henry was fussy about his keys. He always kept a second set on a hook on his belt, in case of emergency. He told people it was in case of an attempted escape, but really it was because one of the lesser guards had mislaid the key to the staff toilet once—an occasion he didn't care to remember.

Henry finished reading about the daring robbery, finished his tea, set down the mug, and sat back, considering what to do next. Eat another cookie, go and taunt some more prisoners, go and shout at the lesser guards, or stay put and get down to a bit of paperwork. He glanced down at his clipboard. The top sheet consisted of a list of names. It was headed *Deportees*.

And then a sharp voice broke into his ruminations. It had a certain bossy, no-nonsense quality that he didn't much like.

"Are you the one to see about bribes?" said the voice.

Henry looked up. A gawky, plain girl with a long, sharp nose, dressed in shabby brown clothes, was staring down at him. She had mousy-brown pigtails. A pencil stuck out of her ugly bonnet. In one hand, she held a basket. She raised an eyebrow, clearly expecting an answer.

Annoyed that he hadn't heard her enter the room, Henry hurriedly removed his feet from the desk. This was a serious breach of security.

"Hey, hey!" said Henry, sitting up straight in a storm of leathery creaking noises. "How did you get in here?"

"Through the secret tunnel from fairyland. Slid down a rainbow. How do you think?"

"And exactly who might you be, missy?"

"My name is Pridy. *P-r-i-d-y.* You're the Head Jailer, right? So you're the one I pay. I'm here to buy my father out. His name is Patrick Pridy. How much?"

The girl rummaged in her basket and brought out a small drawstring purse.

"Well, well, well," sneered Henry unpleasantly. "So you're the little poacher's daughter, eh? I should'ave guessed, with that nose. Well, well, well."

"His name's on tonight's list of deportees." Prudence pointed at the clipboard. "In fact, I can see it there. Right at the bottom. There, see?"

Prudence pointed to Henry's clipboard.

"Hey, hey!" growled Henry, snatching up the clipboard and hugging it to his leather chest. "That list's none o' your business. You shouldn't even be in here."

"Neither should my dad. There's clearly been some mistake. They normally just stick him in the cell at Slopover for a night or two. You can't deport him; he hasn't done anything."

"Oh, is that *so*? You're saying the law got it wrong, are you?"

"Well, yes. Obviously. Oh, come on, you can't be serious. All right, so he does a bit of poaching now and then. He puts food on the table. He's not dangerous. Unless you're furry or feathery."

"Well, Miss Smartyboots, I can tell you that the law's been tightened up. Poaching's been made a deportable offense."

"Which is why I'm here to get him out. Look, let's stop messing around and get to the point. How much will it take to have his name removed and let him slip out the back way?"

There came the sound of footsteps hurrying down a corridor, and a red-faced guard came skidding into the room, all flustered.

"Sorry, Mr. Stumping," gasped the guard. "I

didn't know she was here. I told her to wait at the big gates while I found the visitors' book so I could sign her in, like you said, but she was off down the passage before I—"

"Arthur, you sorry little worm," said Henry. "Get out. I'm talking private business. Wait outside."

"Right away, Mr. Stumping. Sorry," said Arthur the sorry little worm, and got out.

Prudence and Stumping eyed each other steadily over the table.

"So," said Prudence. "How much?"

"Let me get this straight," said Stumping. "You're offerin' me a bribe to alter official paperwork and free a convicted felon? Against the magistrate's orders?"

"Yes. How much?"

Henry eyed the purse thoughtfully, licked his lips, then said, "How much have you got?"

"Two shillings and seven pence," said Prudence through dry lips, and waited with bated breath for the response.

When it came, it was a bad one.

"Oh, dear," sneered Henry, shaking his head. "Not enough. Not by a long shot. I don't come that cheap." He grinned and leaned forward. "And

I'll tell you somethin' else. I wouldn't let yer dad go anyway. Not if you 'ad a 'undred pounds. You know why? Because I don't like you."

"I see," said Prudence. "Not humble enough, I suppose? Should I have cried? Gone down on bended knee?"

"There's that," said Henry, nodding. Then he added, "That and your great big nose."

"And that's your last word?"

"Yep."

"I take it I'm not allowed to see him? To say good-bye?"

"You can do that," said Henry Stumping, nodding again. "One visitor allowed on deportation night. That's the law. It'll cost you, though."

"How much?"

"Ooh, let me see now. Shall we say—two shillings and seven pence?"

"How did I know you were going to say that?" said Prudence. Disgusted, she threw her purse on the table. "Take it. Treat yourself to a course at charm school."

Henry swept it up, stuffed it into his leather jacket, and said, "You've got two minutes. Leave your basket here. Arthur! Take Miss Pridy here down to the holding cell. She wants to say good-bye to her good-for-nothin' dad."

Solly and the Prodigy waited on the cobbled dock-side with Betty. Everywhere was hustle and bustle. Tough-looking men with tattoos scampered up and down with ropes and bellowed instructions. The gray sky was a tangled mass of masts and rigging and screaming gulls. Boats of all shapes and sizes jostled for room, bobbing gently on an oily sea. The taverns lining the wharf had their doors open, trying to get a bit of sea breeze before the night's trade, when they would burst at the seams with sailors, dockers, fishermen, fishwives, and anybody else who thought he (or she) was hard enough.

The cart was parked at the end of Deadman's Passage—the dark, winding, sinister alleyway that led between high buildings and past the gates of the County Jail. Where Prudence was, right now, her coconspirators hoped, bribing the Head Jailer.

Solly stood at Betty's front end, stroking her nose to cheer her up. Every so often, she rolled her eyes at him in a reproachful way. It had taken a lot of singing to persuade her to enter Seaport. When she saw the wharf, she went quite shivery. It was clear she wasn't keen on being there.

"I agree, Betty. Seaport's not a very nice place," said Solly.

It wasn't. It smelled fishy. Away from the dock, where the taverns were, the town consisted of a cobbled main street lined with tall, thin buildings. The shops were dingy, their cracked windows displaying fishing gear, ships' instruments, old accordions, and unwanted parrots. Between the houses and behind the shops was a maze of dark, dangerous alleyways.

The Prodigy said nothing.

"The sea's disappointing too. Not a bit like I thought it would be," went on Solly. "I thought it would be blue. Not all scummy and oily and smelling of old haddock."

The Prodigy still said nothing. She was sitting in the driver's seat, fiddling with Miss Bunnikins's whiskers.

"See out there?" Solly pointed to the distant horizon, where a hulking shape floated. Black smoke belched from a smokestack and rose into the sky. Even seen from far away, it held an unmistakable air of doom. "That'll be the prison ship. It's waiting for the tide to turn."

Still the Prodigy said nothing.

"Prudence is taking her time, isn't she?" fretted

Solly. "I hope she's all right. Suppose she rubs them the wrong way and they arrest her? They can do that, you know. Or can they?"

"Miss Bunnikins's ear's floppin'," announced the Prodigy. "It won't stand up."

"I don't think the bribe's worked. She'd be back by now if it had."

"I don't like it all floppy."

"I hope she's being polite. I did tell her. But you know what she's like. So . . . brisk. It puts people off."

"She's all dirty, too. Her stuffin's all lumpy. An' her eye's comin' loose."

"Is it? I can't say I noticed—oh, I *see*. You're talking about the rabbit."

"Yes," said the Prodigy. "She isn't so bootiful now. Look, some stitches are comin' out. Mr. Skippy didn't have stitches."

"Something's up. They're keeping her in—I just know it."

"I miss Mr. Skippy," the Prodigy continued sadly. "An' I *do* love him."

"One of us should have gone in with her."

"I love him more 'n Miss Bunnikins. I wish he was here."

"She's so stubborn sometimes. We should have insisted."

"Shall I pull her eye out?"

"No. What? Yes. I don't care. Oh, where *is* she?"

"Here," said a voice. And Prudence stepped out of the alley.

She had a funny look on her face. Half furious and half happy, if there could be such a thing. And her unfortunate nose was redder than Solly had ever seen it.

"How'd it go?"

"Not good. I saw the Head Jailer. The man was a pig. He laughed in my face."

"You see?" said the Prodigy to Solly. "I knew she wouldn't do it pwop'ly."

Solly gave her a warning look, but the Prodigy added defiantly, "Well, I *did*. Stop glarwin' at me, Solly."

"She's right," admitted Prudence. "I did it all wrong. People aren't my strong point. There. I've said it. But at least I got to see Dad."

"You did?"

"Yep. It cost me everything I had, and I only had two minutes, but still."

"What's it like in there?" asked Solly.

"Horrible. Long, drippy passages and gates and steps everywhere."

"Skeletons?" whispered the Prodigy hopefully.

"Don't be silly," said Prudence. "They've got him down in the deepest cell. There were others there, but I didn't see them. The guard waited while I spoke to him through the bars."

"How is he?"

"All right. Complaining about the food. Says it can't hold a candle to Ma's cooking. Told me a funny story about a dwarf who shared his cell."

"Dwarf?" said the Prodigy. "What dwarf?"

"Yes," said Solly. "What dwarf?"

"Just some dwarf who was in for being drunk and disorderly. They spent all night showing each other parlor tricks. It's not important. The main thing is, I managed to tell him about the backup plan."

"Excellent!" whooped Solly. "That'll make all the difference."

"The guard was there, so I couldn't say much. I whispered, 'Be ready,' that's all. But he winked. So he knows something's up."

"Good," said Solly. "That should make things a lot easier. So. Let's run through it again, so we're all clear what we're doing. It's all about timing. The ship docks. People start gathering to watch the prisoners go onboard. We go to our places. The jail doors open and the prisoners start off down the alley. That's when Rosabella does her thing. Right, Rosabella?"

"Wight."

"At this point, I'm hiding at the far end of Dead—the passage, behind the water trough. As soon as the diversion's up and running, I'll do the bit with the knife. And Prudence will be waiting with Betty."

"I'm not sure you should do the knife bit," said Prudence doubtfully. "I think *I* should—"

"I'm doing it. We've already agreed. I'm quicker."

"But he's *my* dad!"

"Exactly. You're too involved. You'll get all flustered and mess it up."

"No, I wo—"

"For goodness' sake, stop arguing. *I'm* doing it. So give me the knife, while we're thinking about it. Please."

Prudence rummaged in her basket and produced her useful knife. Solly took it and stuck it in his belt.

"Thanks. Now all we have to do is decide where Rosabella's going to stand." He turned to the Prodigy. "This is your bit, Rosabella. What do you think?"

The Prodigy briefly swept the wharf with her big blue eyes, then she pointed and said with a professional air, "There. On the tub under the gas lamp. Over by the gangplank."

"Right. Anything you need?"

"No. Don't wowwy—I knows what to do. I's good at this."

Annoyingly, she was. Prudence and Solly rolled their eyes at each other.

And now all they could do was wait. Wait for the hazy orange sun to sink into the sea. Wait for dusk to fall and the tide to turn. All three of them looked toward the horizon, where the hulking prison ship waited, silhouetted against a washed-out sky.

"Like a hungry monster, waiting for prey," said Prudence.

She's right, thought Solly. It is.

He wished he could put things as well as Prudence. But then, she was a writer.

THE TIDE TURNS

A chapter full of mist and confusion,

featuring a musical diversion,

an attempted abduction, and,

if you can take the excitement,

more than one daring escape.

The tide turned—and with it came the mist. Great, damp, billowing clouds of it swirled about the prison ship as it slipped into dock. When seen far away on the horizon, the ship had a certain brooding menace. Up close, it wasn't so impressive. Up close, it was a filthy, peeling rust bucket. It arrived silently, nudging the smaller boats to one side, stopping a short way from the landing. It sat there, wheezing black smoke. And then it let out a single, ghostly hoot.

A handful of dockers ran forward with mooring ropes as the gangplank lowered with an ominous clunk.

A crowd had already gathered on the landing and was swelling by the minute. It wasn't quite enough for a proper mob yet, but it was getting that way. Tonight was Deportation Night, and for the more ghoulishly inclined, the wharf was clearly the place to be. The baker's brother, Ted, was right. Throwing eggs and old cauliflowers at convicts was always good for a laugh.

People clutching tankards jammed the doorways of the crowded taverns. Others had stationed themselves midway between Deadman's Passage and the gangplank. These were the ones who liked to get a good view and a clear shot. They were clearly old hands at this, because they made sure they left enough room for the prisoners, who were, after all, the stars of the show. Most were clutching boxes of rotten eggs, buckets of fish heads, and a varied selection of fruit and vegetables. Sadly, a lot of these bystanders were children.

Tsk, tsk.

Suddenly, there was a shrill whistle.

"'Ere they come!" someone shouted. "'Ere come the bad 'uns! Get yer eggs ready!"

A murmur ran through the waiting crowd. Everyone's head craned toward Deadman's Passage. There fell an expectant hush.

And there came a sound. The faint but unmistakable sound of slow, shuffling footsteps approaching. Any minute now the wretched prisoners would appear and walk the gauntlet through the crowd to the waiting ship, under a rain of hurled missiles and rude shouts.

But then . . .

"Good evenin', ladies an' gentlemen," said a

small, high voice. "My name is little Wosabella, an' I's goin' to entertain you wiv a moosical diversion. Yes, I is goin' to sing."

Surprised heads turned. A small girl with golden ringlets and big blue eyes stood on a barrel, over by the gangplank. She was lit by a solitary lamp-post shedding a flattering yellow light that bleached out the grubby stains on her frilly blue frock.

She had a battered blue parasol and a stuffed blue rabbit, which looked rather the worse for wear. Her face wore an angelic expression of pure, sweet, radiant innocence.

"My first song's all 'bout a shipweck, an' evewyone gets dwounded 'cept a dear little boy wiv curls," announced the small girl. "Oh, no, I for-got!" She gave a charming little gasp and rolled her eyes. "He gets dwounded too. Anyways, I hope you like it. I know *I* do. Evewybody gavver wound."

Muttering excitedly, the crowd obediently pressed forward. Who was this enchanting little girl with the lovely manners and the pretty blue dress who was promising entertainment? This was upmarket stuff, for Seaport.

"Closer," encouraged the Prodigy, as more people wandered over from the taverns. "That's wight, fill

up all the gaps. Can evewyone see me? Then I'll begin. It's called 'Dear Little Boy wiv Curls.' Ahem.

"The thunder cwacked, the thunder woared, oh,
    vewy loud it sounded,
The ship was wecked upon the wocks an' all the
    cwew was dwounded,
Except a little boy wiv curls, so vewy bwave
    was he,
All left alone upon the deck to face the wagin'
    seeed. . . ."

The convoy of prisoners shuffled up the narrow alley. There were six of them. They were roped together in single file. Their shoulders were slumped
and they had a dejected air, as well they might.
The sound of the iron door shutting behind them
was still ringing in their ears. There was no turning
back now. It was down to the dock, get mocked by
the mob, be pelted with produce, shuffle onto the
ship, huddle in the hold, and next stop, Black Island. What a fate.

They were accompanied by two guards. The
one at the front was Arthur the sorry little worm.
He had the lantern. The one bringing up the rear
was called Terry. He had a big stick. Neither looked

happy. Nobody liked drawing the short straw on Deportation Night. Too much flying fruit.

The only one of the party who had a certain air of jauntiness was the prisoner at the end of the line. The small, wiry one with the flat cap and the enormous nose. He was looking about him with a nonchalant air that didn't quite sit with his current situation. You got the feeling that he would have had his hands in his pockets, if they hadn't been roped together. He raised his head and casually studied the rooftops. He was even whistling under his breath a bit.

"Lookin' for an escape route, Pridy?" growled the guard at the back (Terry), brandishing his stick. "Hopin' a big bird's gonna come swoopin' down an' carry you away?"

"Ah, no, to be sure, sir," said Paddy Pridy cheerily. "I'm not a popular man with the birds. Just enjoyin' a breath o' night air. Looks like we're in for a bit of a fog."

"Dunno what yer so cheerful about. Wait till you get to Black Island. That'll wipe the smile off yer chops. It's always foggy there. Keep movin'."

"Ah. Now, there I can't help you."

"And why is that?"

"On account o' the party in front of me has stopped."

He was right. The line of prisoners had shuffled to an unexpected halt. Up front, the lantern bobbed, an orange glow in the ever-thickening mist.

"Eh?" Terry looked a bit nonplussed, raised his voice, and shouted, "Oi! Arthur! Wassup?"

"Bit of a blockage," came Arthur's voice from up front. "There's a crowd up ahead, a lot bigger'n usual, jam-packed tight. It's a wall o' backs. We can't get through."

"'Ow d'you mean, can't get through? They're supposed to leave a clear passage to the ship."

"Yeah, well, tonight, they 'aven't. They're listenin' to somethin', I think. Shush."

And from out of the mists it came. A piping treble voice, brimming with pathos and dripping with sentiment.

". . . and so the little boy wiv curls is nuffin'
    more than bones,
I's sad to say he's gone away an' lives wiv Davey
    Jones.
Ooooh, ooooh, he's down wiv Davey Jooooones."

The last strains of the song died away. There was a long silence.

"That's the one who's got the locker," explained the voice, not singing now. "It means he's deaded."

There was another silence. Then, somewhere, a woman wept. Next came scattered clapping. More and more joined in until it was quite an ovation. Over the applause came the unmistakable honking of noses being blown. The Prodigy had touched even the tough hearts of Seaport, which was no mean achievement.

"Lovely!" shouted a tremulous voice, thick with emotion. "Give us another, dearie."

More upraised voices joined in, begging for an encore.

"Get 'em out o' the way, Arthur!" bellowed Terry. "Come on, we'll be here all night!"

"I'm tryin', I'm tryin'! Oi! Move out the way there! Step aside! Queen's official business! Excuse me, missus, do you mind? We're tryin' ter get through!"

The prisoners waited patiently in their line, sunk in their own thoughts, grateful for the short reprieve.

. . .

Back on the wharf, the Prodigy was enjoying herself. Show business was in her blood. Tragic songs were her specialty. She knew how to work an audience. She curtsied and simpered and batted her eyelashes, basking in the applause. Quite a few coins were landing on the barrel, too. Prudence wouldn't approve, of course, but there was no sense in wasting them. Businesslike as always, the Prodigy bent down to scoop them up.

And precisely at that moment, Gross and Shorty arrived on the scene.

They both looked out of sorts, which wasn't surprising considering the miles they had traveled in each other's company. Shorty in particular looked as though he had been having a tough time, which indeed he had. His annoying run of bad luck—blisters, potholes, stinging nettles, falling into ditches, and so on—gave no sign of letting up. But Gross hadn't shown any sympathy, being too tied up with his own problems, and most of the time they had proceeded in silence, each in his own little world of misery.

They had reached Seaport a short time ago, only to find the main street dark and deserted. Gross had made inquiries of a passing lamplighter, who muttered something about everyone being down at the landing before scuttling off home.

So Gross had set off, with Shorty limping sulkily in his wake.

In contrast with the rest of the town, the landing was heaving with people. They were mainly concentrated around the gangplank of a large, waiting ship whose topmast was lost in the clouds of mist that rolled in from the sea. Shadowy figures could be dimly seen on deck, peering from behind bobbing lanterns.

"What's goin' on?" wondered Gross, staring in puzzlement at the sea of backs.

"Prison ship," muttered Shorty. "Traditional sendoff for the prisoners; happens every Friday. Can we sit down for a bit? Got a nasty thorn in me toe."

"Stop grumblin'," said Gross. "I'm tired o' you moanin' all the time."

"I've just walked ten miles in bare feet, pal!" snapped Shorty.

This was true. He had torn strips off his trousers to bind them up, but the method hadn't proved too successful. Now he had sore feet and ridiculously short trousers. What with that and the pom-pom jacket and the remains of the greasepaint, he was attracting quite a few curious stares—as indeed was Gross.

"I said stop complainin'! Come on, let's go nearer. An' keep yer eye open for the little blue girl."

Grimly, Gross grabbed Shorty's arm and shuffled forward to join the tightly packed crowd.

"This is crazy," grumbled Shorty. "We're wastin' our time. Even if she's here, what are the chances of us seein' her in this crowd? Talk about a needle in a haystack."

And then . . .

"Fank you vewy much," said a clear, high voice over by the gangplank. A small blue figure straightened up. She had a little blue parasol tucked under one arm and a stuffed blue rabbit under the other. Both hands were full of coins, which she proceeded to stuff up her knicker leg.

Gross's eyes bulged. He made a hoarse noise deep in his throat. Slowly, he raised a huge arm and pointed.

"Is that her?" he croaked.

There was no reply from Shorty.

"My next song is called 'The Little Lost Lamb-kin,'" announced the little blue girl.

"Aaah," came the united sigh. "Bless you."

"Oh where is my little lost lambkin?
Where, oh where can he be?"

The crowd listened in enthralled silence, hanging on to every word. There were a great many handkerchiefs in evidence. The Prodigy certainly knew how to milk emotion.

"It *is* her, ain't it?" gasped Gross. "She's blue an' she's singin' an' she's got a rabbit—"

"He's all alone on the cliff top . . ."

Still no reply from Shorty.

"We gotta get through," said Gross. "We gotta get 'er!"

"Where the wocks plunge down to the
seeeeaa. . . ."

Gross looked down.

Shorty had disappeared.

Back in Deadman's Passage, Terry was losing his patience.

"Come on, Arthur!" he shouted. "Let's get this show on the road! What you doin' up there?"

"Tryin' to get through. What d'you think?" came the irritable reply.

"Well, get a move on. I got a pot o' tea brewin' back in the guards' room. It'll be meltin' the spoon by now."

"Well, come up here and help, then. I can't budge 'em."

"I dunno," sighed Terry. "If you want somethin' done, do it yerself. Stand aside, you 'orrible lot. I'm comin' through. Outta the way—look sharp."

Obediently, the waiting prisoners shuffled to one side of the narrow alley. Stick in hand, Terry marched purposefully to the front of the line and joined Arthur at the wall of backs.

"See what I mean?" said Arthur. "Packed solid."

"Not for long, though," said Terry, who was made of sterner stuff. "Oi! You! Outta the way; we're comin' through!" And purposefully he raised his stick.

Behind them, the line of drooping prisoners waited, shivering in the damp, swirling darkness, scratching dolefully at itching noses with bound hands and rubbing their chafed ankles. Only the prisoner at the end of the line was alert. He kept glancing around with expectant eyes, casting furtive little looks over his shoulder, back along the alley where the clammy mist hung about most thickly.

And then it happened. A dark shape emerged from the mist. Keeping close to the wall, where the shadows were deepest, it crept forward in a stealthy half crouch, finally revealing itself to be a boy. A ragged boy with a finger to his lips and a useful knife in his hand.

Only Paddy Pridy saw Solly coming. The rest of the prisoners were facing the other way. The real, exciting action was up at the front, where the guards were still attempting to force a passage through the uncooperative crowd, using the time-honored method of bellowing and waving a stick in a threatening manner.

Nobody saw Paddy Pridy's relieved grin as the knife did its work and the ropes fell away, first from his hands and then from his ankles.

Nobody noticed him back silently away, rubbing his wrists, then turn and flee back up the alley, where both he and his rescuer were immediately swallowed by mist and shadows.

There's a Gweat Big Ogre Man!

❧

In which there is a great deal of
blundering around in fog, and a speedy
getaway proves difficult owing to
an unexpected delay.

Prudence sat in the driver's seat of the cart, gnawing on her pencil and trying not to feel resentful. She wasn't enjoying the role of getaway driver. But somebody had to do it. The Prodigy was taking care of the diversion, and Solly had insisted on performing the critical rescue. It had been his idea, so Prudence had had no choice but to agree. That left the one job. Waiting with Betty on a side street and being ready to leave at a moment's notice. Boring. Chilly too, with the mist coming in off the sea.

She shivered and pulled her thin cloak tighter. It was spooky here, parked in the shadows just off the deserted main street, knowing that the real action was going on elsewhere. Prudence hated being sidelined.

But sometimes you have to take a backseat, Prudence told herself. You have to let people do what they're good at. Teamwork. That's the thing.

The trouble was, she was bossy by nature. It didn't come easy.

The mist rolled and coiled up the street. It was getting thicker by the minute. In a way, that was good. It would make pursuit that more difficult. And they would be pursued, of course. At some point, someone would notice they were a prisoner short. But hopefully, not right away. Hopefully, everyone would make it back to the cart. Hopefully, they would have a head start. Hopefully, there would be time to get out of Seaport and onto the open road.

So many *hopefullys*, thought Prudence.

And then what? Back home to Boring—what else? Of course, even then they wouldn't be home safe. Escape from the County Jail wouldn't be treated lightly. Officials would come looking. It would never end. Paddy Pridy wouldn't be safe in his own home ever again.

He'll have to hide out in the woods, thought Prudence. I'll help him build a shelter and take him food. I'll read him bits from the paper. I'll work out a visiting schedule, so he can see the girls. Not Cleanliness; he'll be too loud. Ma'll do his washing. He'll sneak home for Sunday lunch. It'll be all right.

Except, of course, it wouldn't. Oh, in a book, it would work out just fine. There would be a pet fox or maybe a tame owl. Her dad would lead a Robin

Hoodish sort of life, under the greenwood tree. There would be starlit nights when they would discuss deep sorts of things. They would eat rabbit kebabs over a cozy fire while they waited for a pardon from the Queen. And she, Prudence, would write a story that would get published and become a bestseller, and they would all end up rich. There would be a happy ending.

But this was real life. What would happen in winter? What if the fox got snappy and the owl turned bad and the pardon didn't come? Where would the money come from for pencils and paper?

Prudence sighed, wishing for the thousandth time that plots in real life worked out as neatly as they do in books.

"This song," announced the Prodigy, "is called the 'Faiwy Funewal.' I does a bootiful dance wiv this one. It's about a little dyin' faiwy who—"

She didn't have time to finish. She was interrupted by rude shouts coming from the vicinity of Deadman's Passage.

"Comin' through! Mind yer backs! Outta the *way*, missus! How many more times—"

From the waiting prison ship, a single, impatient horn blasted out again, like a lovelorn whale.

On deck, the indistinct shapes moved about in the mist, which was getting really thick now, particularly over the water. The ship was preparing to receive the prisoners.

The mob in general wasn't too pleased at the sudden turn of events. Normally, the arrival of the prisoners was the highlight of the evening, but tonight was different. Tonight there was an unexpected warm-up act of the sort of caliber you rarely got in Seaport. Oh, people *wanted* to heckle and shake their fists and throw vegetables, of course, but not just yet. Right now, they were enjoying the novelty of having their hearts broken by a little angel in blue. The timing was bad.

The Prodigy's timing, however, was excellent. The moment she heard the warning shouts and saw the disturbance toward the back of the crowd, she gave a hasty little curtsy and trilled, "Fank you vewy much, an' good night, Seapawt!"

She bent down, scrabbled for the last few coins, scooped them up, hopped off the barrel—and simply melted away into the crowd.

Very few people noticed. Everyone was now facing the other way, directing their hostility at the guards, who were slowly forcing a path through the crush with the hapless prisoners in their wake.

Only one noticed her hasty exit. Determinedly, like a mountain on the move, Gross waded through the massed crowd, shoving people out of his way, following the occasional flash of blue.

"This way!" gasped Solly as he fled through the maze of misty, ill-lit alleyways with Paddy Pridy scuttling hot on his heels.

"Ah, 'tis glad I am to see ye, young Solly," panted Paddy. "And there was me thinkin' I was a goner. Until our Prudence tipped me the wink, that is. O' course, I had no idea you were involved. That makes it a doubly pleasant surprise, to be sure."

"Yes, well, you're welcome. It was nothing."

"Now, now, no need for modesty. You did a good job there, Solly lad. Simple but effective. All that lurking in the shadows. You'd make a fine poacher. I don't say that often."

"Erm—no. Well, thanks."

"Nice touch, using your little circus friend as a diversionary tactic. I take it those were Miss Rosabella's dulcet tones I heard? Yes, I thought so. Well, I must say, this is a real joy. Let me shake you by the hand."

Paddy Pridy stopped in his tracks and solemnly extended a dirty hand. Solly reached out and took it. He was Prudence's dad. It was only polite. Although this wasn't really the time or place.

"Not at all; least I could do. Better hurry on now, if you don't mind." He tried to take his hand back, but Paddy hadn't finished shaking it.

"No, really. You have my eternal gratitude. How are you keepin' these days?"

"Fine. We really need to hurry, Mr. Pridy. This way, I think."

He finally got his hand back and continued on down the alley. Paddy Pridy scurried along at his side.

"Still in the washing business?"

"Yes."

"Ah, well, it's a solid enough trade."

He really does like a chat, reflected Solly. I wish he'd stop talking for one moment and let me think where I'm going.

"I hear you've got a new donkey and cart."

"Yes."

"Fancy."

"No, not really. This wa—hang on, which way was it?"

Solly came to a sudden stop and looked doubtfully about him. The mist was really thick now. More like proper fog.

"And where are we proceeding to now, young Solly?" inquired Paddy, colliding with his back.

"We're making our way to the road leading out of town. Prudence is there, with Betty. The donkey."

"That's my Prue!" cried Paddy proudly. "Ah, what it is to have a brainy daughter. Trust her to come up with a way to save her old dad from being shipped off to Black Island."

"Mmm," said Solly.

"She'll make our fortune one day," went on Paddy Pridy. Suddenly, he felt around on his head. "Ah, now, will you look at that! I've lost me cap."

"Well, we can't go back for it, I'm afraid."

"No? But it was a good cap, that."

"Maybe, but there's no time. We've got to get you out of here. This way, Mr. Pridy. At least, I'm pretty sure it is. . . ."

In the cart, Prudence sat bolt upright. The fog blotted out everything now, but the sound of approaching footsteps was unmistakable.

Could this be them?

"She's around here somewhere—I'm sure of it. . . ." muttered a familiar voice.

"Solly? Dad? Is that you?" called Prudence in a low voice. The footsteps came closer. . . .

And then they were there, looming out of the fog. Betty gave a little whicker of recognition and snuffled at Solly's hair.

"Dad!" said Prudence. A huge, relieved grin spread over her face.

"Prue!" exclaimed Paddy Pridy delightedly. "There y'are, me darlin'. If yer not a sight fer sore eyes!"

"Move over," said Solly, scrambling into the driver's seat. "I'm driving. Mr. Pridy, if you wouldn't mind getting into the back?"

"To be sure," cried Paddy agreeably, and he hopped into the cart with alacrity. "Ah, this is the life," he remarked, rubbing his hands and settling back against the wicker basket as though he were going on vacation. "Home in style, eh? Has anyone got anything to eat? No? Ah, well. What shall we talk about now? How's Ma and the kiddies?"

"Shush," said Prudence. "You've got to keep hidden, Dad. There are some clothes in the washing basket. Lie down and cover yourself up. As soon as Rosabella gets here, we're going to drive you out of town. Oh, where *is* she?"

"She might have gotten lost in the fog," said Solly. "It's really confusing out there. Or maybe she can't get through the crowds down on the landing. I think I'd better go and look."

"Then you'll get lost too. I'll go. You stay with the cart."

"I'll go," offered Paddy.

"Don't be silly, Dad. You're an escapee, remember? Lie down. *I'll* go."

"Prudence," said Solly firmly, "I'm not letting you go off on your own."

"You have to. You're the only one who can start Betty up. The important thing is to get Dad away before they realize he's gone."

"That's my girl," cut in Paddy from the back. He was pulling Old Mother Rust's unmentionables out of the basket and was spreading them over himself. "Always thinking of her old dad. Will you look at these bloomers? Old Mother Rust's, if I'm not mistaken. Ah, well. Any port in a storm, eh?"

"Prudence," said Solly, "I forbid you to get out of this cart."

Now, this was the wrong choice of words. He knew it as soon as they were out of his mouth. Prudence's face was like thunder. Luckily, though, before the storm could break, there came a welcome sound. Muffled tippy-tapping coming toward them and the sound of panicky breathing.

"Solly?" quavered a hesitant voice from out of the fog. "Pwudence? Where is you?"

"Over here!" shouted Solly and Prudence together.

A moment later, a little blue figure emerged from the fog and leaped headfirst into the back of the cart in a flurry of frills and a jingle of coin-stuffed knicker legs.

"Ooof!" complained Paddy from under the underwear. "That's me you're treadin' on, me darlin'."

"Quick!" screeched the Prodigy, all wide-eyed and breathless. "Dwive! There's a gweat big ogre man, an' he's followin' me!"

"What?"

"A gweat big ogre man wiv two heads! He chased me fwough the cwowds, an' he's gonna put me in his sack! Dwive! Dwive, before he gets here!"

"You're lying about the two heads, aren't you?" said Prudence.

"Yes," admitted the Prodigy. "But the west of it's twue. Oh, huwwy, he's comin'!"

Indeed, he was. From somewhere behind came the sound of shuffling big-booted footsteps, relentlessly approaching like impending doom.

"Hurry up, Solly," said Prudence nervously. "I think she's telling the truth."

"Ooooooh!" wailed the Prodigy. "Ooooooh! I am! *Dwive!*"

"All right, I'm doing it. Ahem. *What shall we do with a drunken sailor, what shall we do . . .*"

"That's right," came Paddy's muffled voice from under the clothes. "Sing a song. Keep the spirits up—that's right."

"He's starting the donkey," explained Prudence. "Keep your voice down, Dad. Whatever happens, stay hidden and don't say a word. I mean it, now. Not a word. And, Rosabella, stop making that noise."

"I can't help it! Ooooooh! Huwwy up, Solly— I's fwited!"

"I'm trying, all right? I can't sing when I'm tense. *Way-hay and up she rises . . .* Come on, Betty, for crying out loud. . . ."

Betty's head came up. Her ears pricked up. She was off!

Everyone gave a sigh of relief as the wheels creaked forward. But then . . .

They stopped. The reason they stopped was that a mighty gorilla hand had come out of the mist and gripped the tailboard. Betty strained against it gamely for a moment or two, then gave up the un-equal task and began licking moss off the wall.

A voice said, "Hold it right there." And a moun-tainous bulk came looming, iceberg-like, out of the fog.

"It's him!" wailed the Prodigy. "It's the ogre!"

"Yes," sighed Solly. "Yes, I gathered that."

His weary eyes traveled up the enormous figure. He supposed he should feel frightened, but funnily enough, he didn't. More than anything, he felt an-noyed. Everything had gone right so far. And now some hulking, stubbly person he had never seen in his life was butting in on the action and needlessly complicating things, just as they were on the point of getting away.

"What are you waiting for? Tell him to go away," hissed Prudence, digging Solly in the ribs.

"Why me?"

"Just do it."

"All right, all right. Look," Solly spoke with a certain irritation. "Look, I don't know who you are or what you want, and quite frankly I don't care. We haven't got time for this. We've got washing to deliver. Kindly take your hand off my cart."

"Gimme the bunny," said Gross.

"We haven't got any money."

"Not *money! Bunny!*"

He pointed firmly at Miss Bunnikins, who was clutched in the Prodigy's arms. The Prodigy squealed and backed on her knees into a corner of the cart. A faint grunt of protest came from under the strewn-about clothes.

"Let me get this clear," said Solly, unable to believe his ears. "You want—the rabbit?"

"Yes," said Gross firmly. "I do."

"Is he goin' to *eat* her?" gasped the Prodigy, eyes wide with a sort of fascinated awe, tinged with what could have been horror but equally could have been glee.

"You want a little kid's toy? A great big bloke like you?" said Prudence with a sneer. "You should be ashamed of yourself."

"Not for me," said Gross. "For Master. Hand it over, little blue girl."

"Won't," said the Prodigy spiritedly. She had gotten over her fright and was returning to form. "You can't have Miss Bunnikins! She's mine. He can't, can he, Solly?"

"Well, if it really means that much to him . . ."

"But she's *miiiiiiine!*"

"But you don't even like her much anymore. You said so yourself."

"But I still got to look after her! You said so! You said I was bad for not takin' care of Mr. Skippy! You did!"

"She's right, you know," said Prudence. "We did. It's the principle of the thing."

"I know," said Solly with a sigh. She was right, of course.

"Come on," said Gross. "Hand it over."

"Suppose we say no?" said Solly. "What then?"

Gross's bushy eyebrows drew together. He scratched at his ear.

"I dunno," he said.

"Let's try it, then. *No.*"

"That's right," said Prudence. "The rabbit stays with us."

"See?" said the Prodigy, and stuck her tongue out. "You can't have her. So there."

Baffled, Gross stared at the three of them. This wasn't supposed to happen. Master said to get the jewel. Those were his orders. But the jewel was in the rabbit, and the rabbit was clutched tightly in the arms of the little blue girl. And they wouldn't let him have it.

Which meant he would have to take it. He would have to reach over and pinch the little blue girl until she dropped it.

And he didn't want to pinch the pretty little blue girl, with her tear-filled eyes and her tangled curls. He didn't want her to stick her tongue out at him. What to do?

"I don't want to pinch the little blue girl," he blurted out.

"I should think not," said Solly.

"But Master wants the rabbit. How'm I s'posed to—" He broke off. Suddenly, it came to him. It was blissfully simple. "Got it," he said. "Move over."

And with no more ado, he clambered onto the driver's seat, shoving Solly along and nearly pushing Prudence off the other side. He took up the reins and said, "Giddyup, donkey."

Betty remained solidly where she was.

"Just what do you think you're doing?" asked Solly.

"Taking you to Master. Giddyup, donkey. Why isn't she moving?"

"See?" jeered the Prodigy. "You doesn't even know how to start up. You's got to sing about a dwunken sailor in a special, howwible voice."

"I don't know any drunken sailors."

"There you are, then. Solly does."

"Sing it, then," said Gross. He gave Solly a

none-too-gentle nudge. "Go on, do it. I'm in a hurry. I gotta get to the Tower!"

"Tower? What tower?" asked Prudence.

"Never you mind."

"We haven't got time to go to a stupid tower, have we, Solly?"

"Definitely out of our way, I'm afraid," said Solly firmly. "Give me the reins back, please. I'm the driver."

"Look," began Gross, "I'm not arguin'—" And then he broke off. His head jerked up and his eyes bulged. "What's that?"

There were sounds in the fog. Faraway sounds, muffled by mist, coming from the direction of the landing. Shouts. A whistle. Running footsteps.

Then came the urgent clanging of a bell.

"That's coming from the jail," said Prudence. She clutched Solly's arm. "They're sounding the alarm. Go. Now."

"But this idiot won't give me the reins!"

"So? Never mind that! Get us out of here!"

"Yers," agreed Gross nervously. Things were getting out of control. "Gotta get outta here. Let's go! Giddyup, donkey, giddyup!"

The footsteps were getting closer. So were the

shouts. Someone somewhere was shouting something about a cap they'd just found and how someone else ought to go and get the sniffer dogs.

"Sing, Solly, sing!" shouted the girls in unison.

"All *right*! Ahem. *Way-hay and up she rises . . .*"

And they were off.

Danger in the Fog

❧

In which there is more blundering
around, this time on foggy cliff tops,
and the Intelligent Reader learns
where Shorty has been all this time.

Shorty was lost. It seemed impossible to believe, but there it was. His bad luck seemed to be going from bad to worse. For a short time there, he had thought things were looking up. The unexpected appearance of the little blue brat down on the crowded landing meant that Gross was distracted for a few vital moments, giving the dwarf the opportunity he had been waiting for. He had simply melted into the crowd and made a run for it. He was once again a free man, which was something.

But now it had all gone wrong again.

This is how it happened. Once he was clear of the crowds, he had beaten a swift retreat from Seaport, heading for the road inland—or so he thought. But the fog had confused him. It came down like a blanket, blotting out all the familiar landmarks and ruining his sense of direction. Somehow, he had ended up on the wrong road.

He was now stumbling blindly up a steep, narrow track, feeling for every step, arms extended in front of him like a sleepwalker. The track had a lot of potholes, leading past wet gorse bushes and clumps of brambles. From somewhere off to one side, he could hear the distant sound of waves breaking on rocks. A wind was beginning to blow. It seemed that he was up on the cliffs. Not good.

Even worse, a short while ago he had heard the sound of a distant bell. It came from behind him. What was all that about? Was it anything to do with him? Surely not. But it was possible, wasn't it? Maybe the law was on his trail. Maybe somebody had spotted him running across the museum roof and reported it. Maybe tomorrow's papers would issue a description: "Firestone Breakthrough! Police Looking for One-Eyed Dwarf." Could they have followed him all the way to Seaport?

Of course, it might have nothing to do with him. But either way he was in a bad situation. There was no telling how close the path was to the cliff edge. One false step—that's all it would take. But surely the path had to lead *somewhere*—to a farm or a coastguard's cottage perhaps? Surely there had to be some other living creature in this remote and blasted spot? Someone who could show him the way or even offer him a bed to sleep in for the night?

The fog was getting even thicker now. Shorty pulled his red pom-pom jacket around him and was about to inch forward another step when he heard a new sound. Cart wheels. Hooves. Coming up from behind at a brisk pace. Getting louder.

For one long moment, he froze to the spot. Whatever it was was almost upon him!

He threw himself to the side and rolled under a gorse bush just in time. He had a glimpse of whirling spokes before the fog swirled back, blotting out all vision.

"What was that?" shouted Prudence, clinging to the edge of the plank as the cart jolted and bounced up the rutted track, which went up and down like a scenic railway. To one side, and far below, came the sound of waves crashing on rocks.

The Prodigy was hanging on for dear life in the back, looking as if she were enjoying herself. Every so often, when a wheel went down a particularly deep pothole, there would come strange, muffled noises from beneath the pile of Old Mother Rust's winter unmentionables. Hard though it is to believe, Paddy Pridy had dropped off to sleep.

"What?" bellowed Solly.

"I thought I saw something out there in the fog."

"Did you? I don't know how you can see a thing. I certainly can't. Look, do you *have* to go so fast?"

This last was an appeal to Gross, who was hunched tensely over the reins, eyebrows drawn together in a scowl. He looked strained but determined. He growled, "Master's waitin'," through gritted teeth.

"Who's Master?" inquired the Prodigy from the back of the cart. Her voice joggled up and down in an amusing way, so she said it again: "M-a-a-a-ster."

"That," said Gross, "I am not allowed to say."

"This cart doesn't have a brake, you know!" said Solly. They had reached the top of a slope and were picking up yet more speed as the track plunged downward. They couldn't see, of course, but their stomachs told them. "Whoa, Betty, take it easy! Look, let *me* drive, why don't you?"

"I's feelin' sick," announced the Prodigy, suddenly looking a bit green. "Si-i-i-ick."

"Can't stop now," said Gross. "Got to get to the Tower."

"That's if we don't go over the cliff first!" snapped Solly. "For crying out loud, give me the *reins.* You're a hopeless driver. You're supposed to drive carefully in fog, not at this crazy speed. Are you mad? What if something's coming the other way? It's all right, Betty—Solly's here."

He leaned over and tried for the hundredth time to snatch back the reins. For the hundredth time, Gross pushed him crossly away and said, "Get off. *I'm* drivin'."

"I's *goin'* to be sick," announced the Prodigy, and she was, over the side of the cart.

Bluuurkk!

"That's all we need," said Prudence grimly.

Bluur-er-er-er-erk!

On and on went the horrible journey over the cliff tops through the fog, to the accompaniment of unpleasant sound effects.

Can anything be worse than this? thought Solly.

Well, yes. Things could.

A stiff breeze blew in off the sea. The fog thinned, a hazy moon drifted out from behind the clouds—

And a tower was before them.

It loomed out of the night, gaunt and forbidding. A massive edifice of black stone, perched right on the edge of the cliff, rearing up endlessly into the night sky. Steep, straight sides, dotted with tiny darkened slit windows. Hazy yellow light shone from the uppermost window. Somebody was there.

"I knew it," said Prudence with a sigh. "I just knew it. Sinister, fogbound, right on the edge of a cliff. Like Cinderella's palace gone bad."

"Home again," said Gross, hauling hard on the reins. Betty came to a relieved halt and stood with her sides heaving. "Come on. All of you get out."

He clambered down and waited expectantly.

"And suppose we say no?" said Solly in steely tones. Well, it had worked once before.

"Get *down*," said Gross grumpily. "Or I'll get you down myself." To hammer home his point, he shook his fist.

"I thought you didn't believe in violence," said Solly.

"I never said that," argued Gross.

"You did. You said you didn't like pinching little girls."

"I don't mind punchin' *you*, though," said Gross. "Get down. I'm not tellin' you again."

The three children exchanged glances. Then, in silence, they got down. Solly immediately went to Betty to make sure she was all right. She gazed at him reproachfully. He gave her a pat, and she licked his ear and blew down her nose.

"Sorry about that," he whispered. She gave an understanding nod and looked about for thistles.

Very carefully, the Prodigy stepped over the piles of strewn-about washing. To everyone's relief, Paddy Pridy did what he was told and lay motionless. (Actually, he was still sleeping, but nobody knew that.)

The Prodigy climbed down, gave Gross a black look, and brushed past with her nose in the air. She didn't look green anymore. Being sick was something she did quite regularly, usually for effect. It didn't bother her, and she always recovered instantly.

Slowly, stiffly, they walked toward the Tower. As they approached, it became obvious that it had seen better days. Some of the buttresses at the base were crumbling. The drainpipes were broken, and the huge wooden doors at the entrance were rotting.

A rusting chain hung at the side. Gross reached out and gave it a tug. Above the sound of waves crashing against the cliff, a sonorous clanging could be heard from within.

Gross stood back, raised his head, cupped his hands to his mouth, and shouted, "Master! It's me! I'm back!"

There was a pause. Then yellow light could be

seen briefly illuminating each window in turn as someone carrying a lamp descended from above.

"Ooooh," said the Prodigy, a little nervous, reaching for Prudence's hand. "Ooooh. Spooky."

"It's ridiculous," said Prudence. "I've never seen anything so overdone." But she let the Prodigy take her hand.

Footsteps could be heard approaching the door. There came the sound of chains being removed and bolts being shot. Then—it opened.

A tall, wild-eyed figure wearing an opera cloak stood dramatically framed in the doorway. He had shoulder-length hair and the beginnings of a small, devilish beard. In his hand was a lantern. The expression on his pale face was a strange mixture of greed, surprise, annoyance, eager anticipation, and several other emotions that would take too long to write down.

He said urgently, "*There* you are, Gross. Tell me quickly, man—do you have it?"

"Yers," said Gross proudly. "I do."

"Thanks be!" cried the wild-eyed one. He fished a white handkerchief from beneath his cloak and mopped his brow, staggering a little. He then recovered, put the handkerchief away, and said furiously,

"Where have you *been*? Have you no idea of punctuality? What kept you?"

"Had a few problems," admitted Gross. "Sorry."

The wild-eyed one transferred his attention to the waiting children. He stared for a long moment, then said nastily, "Well, well. You've brought some little friends. How very *nice*."

"We're not his friends," said Solly grimly. "We don't have anything to do with him. We shouldn't even *be* here."

"That's right," agreed Prudence. "He hijacked our cart."

"What have I always said, Gross?" said the man, ignoring them. "Do not on any account *ever, ever* bring anyone back here. Have I not always said that?"

"Yers," said Gross. "But it's all their fault." He pointed sulkily at the Prodigy. "She wouldn't give me the bunny. An' I didn't want to pinch her, and then the bell started ringin', an' I don't know the drunken sailor."

"Gross," said the man, "what the devil are you talking about?"

"The bunny! The bunny! The one she's holdin' there—look! The dwarf hid the jewel in it. That's what he said. You could ask him yerself, but he runned away."

"Jewel?" said Solly.

"Dwarf?" said Prudence.

"That Shawty," announced the Prodigy suddenly. "I knewed it! I *knewed* he was bad."

"What?" Both Solly and Prudence snapped their heads around.

"That wobbery you was sayin' about. At the mooseum. Shawty done it. That ole dwarf I was sayin' about, wemember? He stoled the jewel and put it in Miss Bunnikins. I knewed he didn't have a paw ole muvver."

"You mean—the Firestone of Toj?" Solly gasped. "All this time we've been carting it round with us, and we never even knew?"

"Right," said Prudence. "So *that's* what this is all about. Quite unknowingly and through no fault of our own, we're tangled up in somebody else's stupid story."

"Where is it, I wonder," went on the Prodigy, quite excited. She held Miss Bunnikins at arm's length, then upended her and began examining her for jewel-shaped lumps. Not for long, though. She gave a surprised little squeal as the man in the cloak reached out and ruthlessly plucked Miss Bunnikins from her arms.

"*I'll* take that," he said.

"Solly!" whined the Prodigy. "Tell him."

Solly hesitated. Both girls were looking at him. It seemed that a bit of heroic action was called for, or at the very least a few strong words. But how to phrase them? Unhand that rabbit? Maybe not.

"Look," he said. "I don't know who you are, mister, but—"

"*Doctor,*" corrected Gross. "He's a doctor. Dr. Calamari, that's his—oops. Sorry." He clapped his hand to his mouth, stared around guiltily, and added, "I wasn't supposed to say that."

He was really falling apart. It was getting increasingly hard to remember what he was and wasn't supposed to say. Tiredness, of course, combined with stress.

"Gross," said Dr. Calamari, "you are a nincompoop."

"Calamari," said Prudence thoughtfully. "That would be Dr. *Casimir* Calamari, well-known recluse and so-called world expert on precious jewels, I take it?"

"What—you know him?" Solly said with a gasp.

"I know *of* him. His name crops up from time

to time in the more boring bits of the newspapers. Am I right, Calamari?"

"Quite often, actually," snapped Dr. Calamari. "And less of the so-called. And it's *Doctor* to you."

"Wow, Prudence," said Solly, filled with admiration. "You really know a lot of stuff."

Well, she did. All that reading really came in handy sometimes.

"Calls himself Doctor," sneered Prudence. "But he's just a common thief."

"Yes," agreed the Prodigy. "An' where's his stifflescope? Weal doctors have stifflescopes."

"Not *that* kind of doctor," snarled Dr. Calamari. "Why do people always assume that? If there's one thing I hate, it's people who *assume* that."

"This is ridiculous," cut in Solly. He had really had enough of standing around talking in fog. They had a getaway to get on with. Mr. Pridy was still in the cart. He would be getting pins and needles by now. At any moment, he could sneeze or something. "Look, keep the stupid toy. We didn't know there was a jewel in it. We don't care, really. It's none of our business."

"Oh, no," said Dr. Calamari. "I'm afraid it's not that simple. You know too much, you see. Step inside. Gross! Bring them up to my turret room."

THE TURRET ROOM

❦

A truly dramatic chapter, featuring

a climax full of surprise revelations.

You will have to concentrate on this one.

T he turret room lay at the top of 162 stairs. Everyone was gasping for breath when they finally reached the top and Dr. Calamari flung open the door.

"In," he ordered.

In they went. Solly first, then Prudence, then the Prodigy, with Gross bringing up the rear.

Solly looked around curiously. The room was cold and stark, with stone walls and flagstones on the floor. Here and there, candles flickered in niches. A book filled with scrawly writing was open on a desk that stood beneath a tall, narrow window, beyond which fog swirled.

Apart from the desk, there was only one item of furniture. A tall, black lacquered cabinet, covered in ornate Oriental designs painted in gold — fire-breathing dragons, mainly. The cabinet stood in the center of the room. A stout padlock hung on the doors.

Dr. Calamari whirled across the room, threw open a desk drawer, and madly began to scrabble in it, muttering, "Scissors, scissors."

"Mad collector," hissed Prudence in Solly's ear.

"What?"

"Well, it's obvious, isn't it? Look at that cabinet. I bet it's full of—"

"That's enough talk!" cried Dr. Calamari. "Gross, where are the wretched scissors? Have you taken the—aha! The letter opener. That will do nicely."

He straightened. In his hand was a long, thin, curved knife with a black lacquered handle. It looked like a free gift that had come with the cabinet.

"Now," said Dr. Calamari, "the moment of truth." And he held Miss Bunnikins up by her ears.

It has to be said that Miss Bunnikins was now sadly lacking in her former allure. Her adventures on the road had taken their toll. She wasn't so blue anymore. Both ears were coming loose. Her blue ribbon was missing, and one eye hung on a single thread. Her seams were coming undone. Her stuffing was exploding out all over the place, and she bulged and sagged in all the wrong places. She still wore her expression of stitched-on happiness, but it didn't ring true.

"Be brave," said Solly, reaching out and giving the Prodigy's hand a squeeze. "She's not real. It won't hurt."

"I know *that*," said the Prodigy scornfully. "It's all wight. I's lost intwest in her, anyway."

Solly and Prudence shook their heads in despair.

"Fickle," said Prudence to Solly.

"Heartless," agreed Solly.

"Well, we can give her a *funewal*," added the Prodigy, as if this made it all right. "I's got a box at home."

And then, just at that critical moment, when the knife was at Miss Bunnikins's throat, there came an interruption. A noise came from far below. A thunderous banging, which echoed up the 162 stairs, bouncing off the walls. At the same time, a bell started jangling.

"Blow, blast, bother, and blast again!" exploded Dr. Calamari. "I just *hate* it when that happens! Gross, go down and answer the door. Whoever it is, get rid of them."

What, again? thought Gross. Those stairs *again*? But he went anyway.

Downstairs, a one-eyed dwarf in a filthy red pompom jacket and ragged trousers was not so much knocking at the door as throwing himself at it, attacking it with his little fists and simultaneously kicking at the panels with his bare feet.

Yes. By an amazing coincidence, our old friend Shorty had arrived at the Tower.

He had been staggering blindly through the fog over the cliffs for a long time. He had seen or heard nothing since the near accident with the cart a while back. Nothing apart from fog and the ever-present sound of the sea. He was scratched, bruised, soaking wet, exhausted, thirsty, and ravenously hungry. And still hopelessly lost.

So imagine his relief when he finally saw the light in the fog. At last! A house!

He stumbled toward the light. Now he could see that it came from the topmost window of a tall black tower rising out of the fog. The donkey cart that had nearly knocked him down earlier was parked to one side. The donkey was chewing a thistle. The cart, rather oddly, contained a wicker basket stuffed with dubious-looking items of underwear. More of the same was strewn about in the bottom of the cart. Shorty went right on past, making for the wooden door that lay ahead.

Directions, thought Shorty. I can get directions. Maybe a nice little old lady lives in there. Maybe she'll give me a warm-up by the fire and a bit of soup. While I'm at it, I'll have a strong word with her about her dangerous driving. Then I'll steal her life's savings, swipe the donkey and cart, and be on my way. Maybe my luck's finally changed.

But it hadn't.

He was just drawing his foot back to give the door another kick when he heard the sound of approaching footsteps. This was followed by clinkings and rattlings. The door opened.

Shorty's eye traveled slowly up. And up. And up a bit more.

He said, "Oh."

That was all he had time for before a huge arm shot out of the darkness and plucked him off his feet. The door shut with an almighty crash.

A moment or two later, over in the cart, Old Mother Rust's unmentionables gave a heave and a sleepy voice murmured, "Put the kettle on, Prue, me darlin'—I'm home!"

Paddy Pridy was waking up.

Up in the turret room, things were getting rather awkward. Nobody was saying anything. Dr. Calamari was a study in nail-biting tension, letter opener in one hand, Miss Bunnikins in the other. Every time anyone coughed or shuffled a bit, he glared and hissed, "Shhhhhh!"

Gross's return came as something of a relief. They heard the sound of footsteps, combined with heavy breathing, then he burst into the room, crying, "Look what I got, Master!"

Shorty was dangling from one huge fist, his little legs paddling the air. His face was very red, and his single blue eye bulged alarmingly.

"Shawty!" squealed the Prodigy. "What's *he* doin' here?"

"Ah," said Dr. Calamari. "The dwarf that got away."

"So that's who robbed the museum," said Prudence. "He doesn't look like much, does he?"

"He's not," sneered the Prodigy with a curl of the lip. "He's a tewwible clown." She pointed her little blue parasol at Shorty and spat venomously, "*Huh! You!* I's tellin' Uncle on *you*."

Shorty said nothing. There are times in life when it is better to be quiet. This was one of them.

"Put him down," ordered Dr. Calamari.

Gross lowered his arm, dumped Shorty on the floor, and stood over him in a threatening manner.

"So, Short," said Dr. Calamari coldly. "We meet at last. Of course, that wasn't in the plan, but circumstances have changed. You are just in time. We are about to reveal the Firestone of Toj, which I gather you placed in this toy rabbit, for some mad reason known only to yourself."

Shorty still said nothing. His single blue eye flickered from side to side, but his lips remained firmly closed.

"Nothing to say?" Dr. Calamari arched his eyebrow. "Well, then, perhaps you might like to tell us why you *ran away*? Without even collecting what is owed you? Odd behavior, to say the least. Are you trying to cheat me, Short? Is that your cunning plan? No? You won't tell us that? Well, then, perhaps you might tell us—"

"Excuse me?" interrupted Solly.

"What?" snapped Dr. Calamari.

"This is all very interesting, but do you think you could get on with it? It's just that you're asking an awful lot of questions, and it's going to take ages for him to reply. I mean, he's sure to have a long, rambling story to tell. And he hasn't said a single word yet. We'll be here all night at this rate."

"I agree," said Prudence. "Just get the stupid jewel and be done with it."

"You're right," said Dr. Calamari. "I've waited long enough. Are you standing comfortably? Then I'll begin. Carving time!"

The letter opener flashed—there was a collective gasp—and suddenly the air was full of flying stuffing.

Paddy Pridy was on his way up the stairs when he heard the cry. Well, it was more of a howl. It went, *"Nooooooooooo!"*

"Will you listen to that!" Paddy gasped. He stopped, hand on thumping heart. Until that point, he had taken it easy up the winding staircase. He was still a bit groggy from his nap. The cry was something he could have done without.

On waking, he had been rather surprised to find himself all on his own in the donkey cart, which was parked before a sinister-looking tower on a cliff top. There was no sign of any of the children. No sound of police whistles or dogs either. That was good. Just tower, mist, and the sound of the sea.

The next surprise was that the door of the sinister-looking tower was open wide. Anyone could walk in. Him, for example.

In fact, that's just what he would do. He fancied

a stretch of the legs anyway. And there was a good chance the kiddies were up there.

I'll saunter on up and see if I can finagle a cup of tea, thought Paddy.

But before he could climb down from the cart, he received yet another surprise. As to what that was—well, we must wait and see. For now, all you need to know is that he was currently halfway up the stairs, carrying it in his hand.

Dr. Calamari stood over the dismembered remains of what was once Miss Bunnikins. His face was a mask of shocked disbelief. Bits of airborne stuffing drifted down to join the sad little pile of ears, buttons, and dirty blue wool. Her expression of bland happiness was no more.

Slowly, the children unscrewed their eyes and took their fingers from their ringing ears. The howl had been unexpected and extremely loud.

"That was horrible," said Prudence coldly. "Please don't do it again."

"It's not in there," said Dr. Calamari.

"I don't believe this," muttered Solly. Not another twist in the plot, surely?

"Wha—" gasped Gross. His jaw dropped open. His eyebrows nearly shot off the top of his head in astonishment.

"You heard me. The Firestone. It's not there. Why isn't it in there, Gross?"

"I dunno," said Gross. He stared stupidly down at the mess on the floor and stirred it with his foot.

"What are you asking him for?" asked Prudence. "It's a waste of time asking him. You should be asking *him*." She pointed to Shorty, who gave her a dirty look.

"Yes," said the Prodigy. She had wandered over to the lacquered cabinet and was breathing on it and writing her name with a finger. "Go on, ask him. Where's the missin' jewel, Shawty, you fief?"

And then . . .

"Anybody hurt?" said a voice. It came unexpectedly from behind. "Thought I heard a howl."

Everyone turned and goggled. Paddy Pridy was standing in the doorway, puffing a bit from the climb. He had an air of pleasant inquiry, as though he were a helpful neighbor who was just popping in to see if there was anything he could pick up from the shops.

That took everyone by complete surprise. But it was nothing compared to the surprise they all got when they saw what he was holding in his hand.

For a split second, you could have heard a pin drop. But only for a split second.

"Mr. Skippy!" screamed the Prodigy, her face lighting up like a pink sunrise. "It's *Mr. Skippy!*"

And she hurtled across the room, seized hold of her beloved, and wrapped him in a stifling blue embrace.

"What *now*?" said Dr. Calamari testily.

"Wonders will never cease!" Prudence gasped. "It is! It *is* Mr. Skippy!"

"Everyone can see him, then?" inquired Solly hopefully. "It's not just me going mad?"

"No, it's him all right," said Prudence. "Those droopy ears. That blank stare. Look how boring he is. Unmistakable."

"Hooway!" cried the Prodigy, dancing around and showering the unresponsive brown head with kisses. "I's missed you, Mr. Skippy. I loves you *lots*!"

"Hiding at the bottom of the washing basket, he was," explained Paddy to the assembled company. "Gave me a bit of a turn when his head popped up. Thought it was the Ghost of Rabbits Past, come to claim revenge. Only for a moment, mind you. Then I saw it was Miss Rosabella's little pet."

"Excuse *me*," cut in Dr. Calamari snappishly. "Would somebody kindly explain what is going on here? Who is this man and why is he here?"

"That's my father," said Prudence. "He was

supposed to stay hidden in the cart. Weren't you, Dad?"

This last was directed at Paddy, who looked cheerfully rueful and muttered something about leg stretching and a cup of tea.

"I *see*," said Dr. Calamari with poisonous sarcasm. "And people do that, do they? Ride around with *fathers* hidden in *carts*? Did you know about this, Gross? Were you aware that there was a *father* hiding in the cart?"

"No," confessed Gross. He added mysteriously, "He musta been under the—you know—ladies' underpants."

"Underpants?"

Dr. Calamari's face was such a picture of incomprehension that Solly almost felt sorry for him. But not quite.

"Look," he said, "none of this matters to you, does it? Fathers, underpants . . . Why do you care what we keep in the cart? Shouldn't you be getting back to the main business? We still don't know what happened to the Firestone, do we? I don't know about anyone else, but I'm curious to get to the bottom of it. Aren't you, Prudence?"

"I suppose I am, a bit," admitted Prudence. "Now that we've come this far."

"I loves you, Mr. Skippy," sang the Prodigy, skipping around, oblivious to anything but the furry brown lump in her arms. She didn't even notice that she was callously skipping through the litter of shredded blue wool and cotton waste that was once Miss Bunnikins. Sadly, she was that sort of child.

"You know, boy, you're right," agreed Dr. Calamari. "There have been quite enough distractions. Back to the matter at hand."

He took two strides toward Shorty, stooped down, and poked a finger at his chest.

"Where is it, Short?" he hissed. "Where is the Firestone of Toj? Tell me now, or—"

"Hey!" said a voice. It belonged to Paddy Pridy. He was pointing at Shorty with a look of amazed recognition. "Hey, little feller there! Don't I know you?"

"What?" said everyone in chorus.

"No," lied Shorty. "Never seen you in me life."

These were the first words he had said. They were delivered in a mutinous mutter, accompanied by a dark, rebellious glare.

"Ah, but I do!" cried Paddy. "Sure, and we shared the same cell a while back. You were in for the night, remember? Paddy Pridy. You must remember me!"

"That wasn't me," said Shorty. He licked his lips, and his eye darted about. "That was someone else."

"Don't be so silly," interjected Prudence. "How many one-eyed dwarfs are there running around? Of course it was you."

"Sure an' it was," confirmed Paddy. "Shorty. That was the name; it's just come to me. You were in for bein' drunk an' disorderly. Had a lot to say for yerself. Told me all about the burglin' business. Let me in on a few trade secrets, as I recall."

"I dunno what you're talkin' about!" burst out Shorty suddenly. "An' I dunno why the jewel ain't in the rabbit either! It musta fallen out. Or someone pinched it. What about her?" He waved an accusing arm at the Prodigy. "*She* coulda taken it. Anyone could have. Why go blamin' me?"

"Cuz nobody likes you," said the Prodigy promptly. "*We* don't like him, do we, Mr. Skippy?"

Mr. Skippy gave one of his funny little shivers.

"I still don't know why the little feller's makin' out he doesn't know me," Paddy informed the room in general. "Come on; you must remember. You showed me that thing you do with the eye. Had me goin' there for a minute."

"What thing with the eye?" asked Solly.

"Ah, well, you see, he does a little trick with—"

"Enough!" exploded Dr. Calamari. "I don't want to hear about eye trickery! All I care about is the Firestone! Short, you're a liar. Don't think you can pull the wool over my eyes. I think you know exactly where that jewel is, and I intend to find it. Empty your pockets!"

"Solly," said the Prodigy suddenly, "Mr. Skippy's actin' funny. He's goin' all wiggly."

"Put him down, then," said Solly vaguely.

The Prodigy put Mr. Skippy down. Right in the middle of the pile of stuffing that used to be Miss Bunnikins.

Close examination would have revealed that he then began acting very strangely indeed. Instead of just plunking down and staring into space, he seemed out of sorts. His nose was twitching frantically, and those funny little shivers were running through his body. Not that anyone noticed. There was too much else going on.

"Come along, Short," insisted Dr. Calamari. "Empty your—"

"Shhhh!" said Solly suddenly. "Wait! What's that?"

He had heard something from outside. A whistle. Distant shouts. A barking dog.

He wiggled his eyebrows frantically at Prudence, whose nose had gone bright red. They were both thinking the same thing. Could this be the search party from the prison, finally homing in on Mr. Pridy?

And then it happened. Shorty made his move. He lunged to one side. Gross shot out a hand. There came the sound of tearing cloth, the collar of his little red jacket was left behind in Gross's hand, and Shorty was skidding wildly across the room toward the door.

"Stop him!" howled Dr. Calamari. "He's getting away!"

He nearly did, too. He almost made it to the door. But he hadn't reckoned on Mr. Skippy.

His foot collided with the furry body, and with a little cry, he pitched forward and landed flat on his face on the floor. And something rolled out of his pocket. Something small and round, like a marble. Everyone's eyes followed this interesting object as it rolled across the floor, pinged off the lacquered cabinet, then rolled back again, ending up at Solly's foot.

"Well, well," said Solly. "Will you look at that?" He stooped, picked up the object, and held it out for everyone to see.

Was it the Firestone? Was it that glorious, price-less, ancient red ruby?

No. It was a blue, staring glass eye.

"Yuck," said Prudence and the Prodigy together.

"You see?" cried Paddy. "That's the thing I was tellin' you about. He can take his eye out! Some trick, eh?"

Just at that moment, there came the sound of a door banging far below, followed by the sound of footsteps running up stairs.

"Gross," hissed Dr. Calamari wildly, "what's going on?"

Gross gave a hopeless shrug. He had lost the plot a long time ago.

"That'll be the search party coming after Dad," said Prudence.

"Ah, well," said Paddy Pridy, a bit subdued. "I suppose it had to happen. It's Black Island for me, then."

Prudence stamped her foot furiously. "See what you've done, Calamari? You've ruined everything! We had it all worked out, then you come along and mess it all up with your daft plan and your stupid stolen jewel, which you can't even find, and your—"

There would have been a lot more of the same thing if it hadn't been for the interruption. The door burst open with a crash, and Arthur and Terry ran in. Arthur had a flaming torch, and Terry had his big stick. He had also acquired a small, yapping dog from somewhere, which he held on a leash.

"Stop, in the name of the—" began Arthur.

"All right, Arthur, I'll do this," said Terry. He pointed his stick at Paddy. "Pridy, you're under arrest. And don't try any funny business."

"Ah, well," said Paddy with a little sigh. "I thought it was all a bit too good to be true. I'll go quietly; it's only fair."

"No, it isn't," argued Prudence. "It isn't fair at all. You stay right where you are, Dad."

The small, yapping dog had spotted Mr. Skippy, who was still crouched among Miss Bunnikins's remains. The dog strained at the leash. Mr. Skippy stared straight ahead and didn't move a muscle. The Prodigy scooped him up protectively.

"Excuse *me*," came the voice of Dr. Calamari. It sounded rather shrill. "*Do* you mind? This is *my* tower. You can't just come barging in here. Do you know who I am?"

"Yes, sir," said Arthur, tugging his forelock. "You're that famous doctor gentleman with the long name."

"Really?" said Terry. "That's handy. It's just that I've got this really sore place on my b—"

"STOP!" shouted Solly at the top of his voice. All of a sudden, he'd had enough. It was time to get to the bottom of this.

Rather to his surprise, everyone went silent.

"This is getting us nowhere," he said. "Let's deal with one thing at a time. We all want to know where the jewel is, right?"

"Right," chorused everybody except Arthur and Terry, who looked confused and said, "What?"

"Well," said Solly, "first, we'll get that sorted out. Let's just see if my hunch is right."

And he marched over to Shorty, pulled off his eye patch—

And the Firestone of Toj fell into his hand.

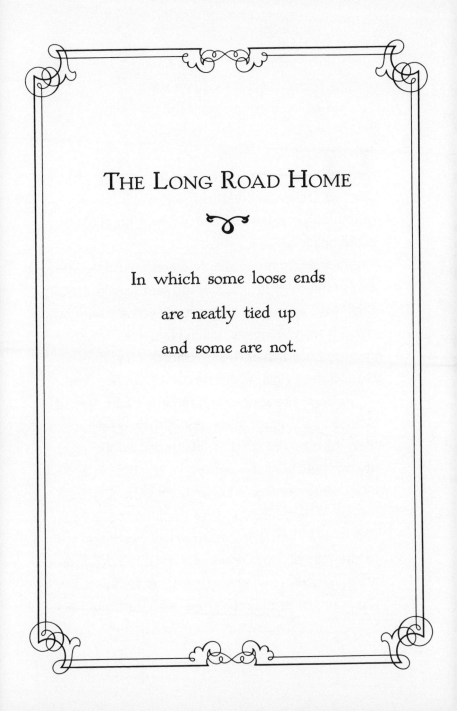

THE LONG ROAD HOME

In which some loose ends

are neatly tied up

and some are not.

Here we all are, then," said Solly. "Blue sky, sun shining, and we're on our way home. What could be nicer?"

They were rattling slowly down a narrow country lane, past hedges and fields and dappled trees. Birds were singing. It was a bright morning with no sign of fog. Betty was taking her time, stopping every so often to munch a bit of hedge that took her fancy. Solly let her. There was no hurry. Not now.

Paddy Pridy sat in the back of the cart, staring around at the passing scenery, giving appreciative little sniffs of the good, fresh country air. Every so often he would pat his pocket, in which there was a clean white envelope containing his official pardon.

Yes, folks! Things were looking up. Paddy had been let off. The Firestone had been returned to the museum, and there was even talk of a reward. Maybe a proper ceremony, up in Town. Dr. Calamari was helping the police with their inquiries. Shorty had been arrested. Gross had disappeared—

nobody knew where to, but it was to be hoped that he would find himself a better master than the last one. Finally, they could all go home—the Prodigy to the circus and everyone else back to Boring. What could be better?

The three children sat up front. Mr. Skippy was back in his usual place, on the Prodigy's lap. Prudence was reading *The Mysterious Case of the Missing Diamond Necklace*.

Solly nudged her in the ribs.

"What?" said Prudence.

"I was just saying I'm glad it's all over and we're going home. Aren't you?"

"Yes. Look, I'm on the last two pages. I want to find out how it ends."

"I don't know why you want to read about made-up missing jewels when we've just found a real one. I suppose it's all over the papers. Us finding the Firestone. Do you think it'll be all over the papers? Shall we stop off at a village somewhere and get a paper?"

"No," said Prudence with her nose back in the book. "Let's just go home."

"Yes," said the Prodigy, yawning a bit. "Let's."

She didn't even mention sweets, thought Solly. She *must* be tired.

"Just think," he said. "My name in the paper."

"Mm," said Prudence.

"I wish I could read it," he added, a bit wistfully.

"I've told you I'll teach you, when there's time," promised Prudence. She added, "It shouldn't take long. It's not as if you haven't got brains."

"Do you think I've got brains?" said Solly, surprised.

"Of course. It was your plan that got Dad out. And you worked out where the Firestone was before anyone else."

"But Mr. Skippy helped, didn't he?" broke in the Prodigy. "Cuz he twipped Shawty up."

"Certainly he helped," agreed Solly.

Everyone looked at Mr. Skippy, who was staring out at the passing hedges, his face a mask of indifference.

"Mr. Skippy," mused Solly. "I've worked out a lot of things in my head, but I'm still not clear how he fits in. Where did he come from? How did he get in the cart? When did he get in the cart? *Why* did he get in the cart?"

"He was followin' me," said the Prodigy, fondly nuzzling the bored brown furry head. "He was followin' me cuz he loves me."

"Or maybe," suggested Prudence, snickering a bit, "maybe he loved Miss Bunnikins."

"I hope not," said Solly. He felt quite shocked. "If that's the case, it's a terrible thing for him to have seen. His loved one, all chopped up and inside out and spread all over the place. Do you really think . . ."

"No," said Prudence. "I was joking. Of course he didn't love her. She's *knitted,* for crying out loud. Even *he's* not that stupid, surely."

"Did you, Mr. Skippy?" asked the Prodigy, stroking the floppy ears. "Did you love Miss Bunnikins?"

Mr. Skippy stared straight ahead. If he had any feelings on the matter, he was keeping them to himself. They would never know.

"I'll give 'im a cawwot when we get back to the circus," said the Prodigy. "To cheer 'im up. He'll be all wight."

"What do you think will happen to Dr. Calamari?" said Solly. "Do you think he'll end up behind bars?"

"No doubt about it," said Prudence. "He was the mastermind behind it all. He can hardly deny it, can he? It's all written down in his journal. And apparently that cabinet of his was packed with stolen stuff. I'd like to have been there when they opened it."

"The Cabinet of Doctor Calamari," mused Solly. "It would make a good name for a book, don't you think?"

"That ole Shawty'll go to pwison, anyway," chipped in the Prodigy. She added gleefully, "Good. I can't wait to tell Miss Pandowa Constantinople." She stuck her thumb in her mouth and snuggled up to Prudence, who pushed her away and said, "Get off. I'm *reading*. Look, can we stop talking, just for one minute? I want to get to the end."

"All right," agreed Solly. It seemed fair enough. There was a pause. He hummed a snatch of 'What Shall We Do with a Drunken Sailor?' Betty sped up a fraction. Then—

"Finished," said Prudence, snapping the book shut.

"So who did it?" asked Solly.

"Billy Grubb. The gardener."

"I thought he had an iron-clad alibi."

"He did. It's a long story. It wasn't that good after all, actually. Not much action. No jokes. I think I prefer adventure stories after all."

"Me, too," agreed Solly. "Hey, I've just thought of an idea for your next book. You could base it on us.

It's got all the right ingredients. Stolen jewel, daring escape from prison, mad ride over fogbound cliffs. Evil mastermind. Bent dwarf. Songs. A royal pardon. And hopefully a decent reward, which should make a reasonably happy ending. What about that for a story? You could write that, couldn't you?"

"I could," said Prudence. "But nobody would believe it."

Don't miss the original adventures
of Solomon Snow!

Solomon Snow
and the Silver Spoon

In which the Intelligent Reader

joins Solly and the gang on a quest

to discover the truth of his parentage.

ISBN 978-0-7636-3218-2